Return To Heaven

OTHER BOOKS BY JIM FEAZELL

"COME THE SWINE"
A SUPERNATURAL THRILLER

"DRY HEAT"
A POLICE DRAMA

"THE LORD'S SHARE"
A LOVE TO KILL FOR

Dual Novelettes
"THE LEGEND OF CAT MOUNTAIN"
A SUPERNATURAL MYSTERY
and
"THE TROUBLE WITH RODNEY"
A SUPERNATURAL MYSTERY

Available from iuniverse.com
or any online book seller

THANKS FOR YOUR SUPPORT

Return To Heaven

JIM FEAZELL

iUniverse, Inc.
New York   Bloomington

iUniverse books may be ordered through booksellers or by contacting:

*iUniverse
1663 Liberty Drive
Bloomington, IN 47403
www.iuniverse.com
1-800-Authors (1-800-288-4677)*

*Because of the dynamic nature of the Internet, any Web addresses or
links contained in this book may have changed since publication and
may no longer be valid. The views expressed in this work are solely those
of the author and do not necessarily reflect the views of the publisher,
and the publisher hereby disclaims any responsibility for them.*

*ISBN: 978-1-4401-7661-6 (sc)
ISBN: 978-1-4401-7662-3 (ebook)*

Printed in the United States of America

iUniverse rev. date: 11/10/2009

For my very good friend,
T. K. LAMEY

Prologue

The young lady with shaggy cropped black hair, erratic bangs, and a distinctive worried look, left El Dorado, drove under an overpass, passed the turnoff to Little Rock, went under another overpass, and found herself on highway 7 headed northwest. Some ten or twelve miles up the highway, a sudden feeling of foreboding anxiety overtook her as an old faded sign loomed at her from the side of the road.

The sign read HEAVEN, population 1250. The 1250 was crossed out and under it written in spray paint was 950. An arrow pointed to the right. She made the right turn onto the old highway 7.

On this cool and not so unusual overcast day the west wind had picked up and begun to rustle the trees, dropping small limbs and pinecones on the narrow meandering blacktop road. She drove the white Grand Prix slowly through the dense eerie woods for another couple of miles where she came upon a large area of cleared land on the right. The blacktop road forked as the old highway continued to the left and another sign with an arrow and the name HEAVEN, pointed to the right.

She took the right and kept driving. Wishing to make a good impression, she wore trendy denim ¾ length trousers, a white silk blouse and a luxurious burnt orange gabardine evening jacket. As she entered town and passed a church, a cemetery and a few old large antebellum homes she began to hear intermittent swishing sounds like gusts of wind and eerie screaming, alike to that of female screams passing over the car and circling around overhead. And laughter. Ungodly weird frightening female laughter.

Trembling nervously and afraid to look up, she continued to drive until she passed a traffic light where she then parked parallel on the left beside some other cars next to a large stand of big oak trees. It was fast approaching dark and through the trees she could see lights on in a building. She continued to hear the sounds circling overhead and she knew there was one of whatever it was on top of the car. She could hear it scratching. Then suddenly it appeared on the hood and looked through the windshield. A totally nude, beautiful redheaded young woman, with huge black wings. She scratched on the windshield, smiled, bared her fangs and laughed deeply and rapturously. The young lady in the car began to scream hysterically. She soon stopped screaming and noticed the thing on her hood had left, as had the others that were flying around overhead. She responded to a light tapping on her side window glass.

The man that tapped on her window was a handsome young man in a dark suit and white shirt with open collar He smiled at her and told her the monsters were gone. To her, he was a knight in shining armor. Her savior. Trembling, she opened the car door and stepped out. She was reluctant and tried to pull away when the man held her close to him. "*You're trembling.*" he said in a soft, yet strong and articulate voice. "*Let me warm you.*" He pulled her closer to him. She was frightened and tried to pull free. He lifted her and held her tight against the car. She could feel his hardness against her as she watched his eyes glow yellowish-red. His mouth opened wide and his salivating fangs protruded as he pushed her head back revealing her soft white neck. She tried to scream but it did not come. The immense fear was to much for her. Her mind shut down and she passed out as he leaned his dripping mouth in toward her neck. His three naked brides flew around in a circle above squawking like a flock of vultures awaiting the kill. They screamed loudly.

"*Bite her, Victor*"—"*Bite her, Victor*"—"*Bite her.*"

Chapter 1

The Troubadour tonight takes great pleasure in welcoming for your listening pleasure. The incomparable Mister Chuck Abbot—the third.

The house lights went down and the spot light came up on Chuck.

"Hello." he said. "I'm Chuck Abbott, and he began to play the guitar and sing a heavy-hearted folk ballad.

"Up the river.. around the bend..
don't reckon I'll go back again..
to where I met Amanda Jane...
in the field by the sugar cane...

The sweetest time
I've ever known...
was that moment we were alone..
as sure as the sun shines above...
she was meant to be my love...

Amanda Jane....Amanda Jane....
you whispered my name...

....Amanda Jane....
Amanda Jane....Amanda Jane....
tell me who's to blame.....
....Amanda Jane....

My heart pounded...
my blood ran warm...
as I bathed my soul...
in all her charm...
there in her eyes
like blue in the sea...
was a little tear of love for me...

I wanted to tell her
how much I cared...
when silently our
thoughts were shared...
but what can you say
when you're cutting cane...
up the river......
on a chain gang....

Amanda Jane....Amanda Jane....
you whispered my name...
....Amanda Jane....
Amanda Jane....Amanda Jane....
tell me who's to blame....
....Amanda Jane....

Love for me.. has come to late…
the electric chair's
gonna be my fate…
the warden told me early today…
the man I shot…passed away…..

Up the river.. around the bend..
don't recon I'll go back again..
to where I met Amanda Jane…
in the field by the sugar cane…

Amanda Jane…. Amanda Jane….
you whispered my name…
….Amanda Jane….
Amanda Jane….Amanda Jane….
tell me who's to blame….
….Amanda Jane…."

Chuck had a good following as an entertainer. He performed regular whenever time permitted between acting engagements. He especially liked the Troubadour club. Susie was always there leading the cheering section.

He had for the past couple of years, organized and copyrighted all of his, or his grandfathers, old songs. He talked the other day to a producer, Pete Anderson, from a major record label about handling him as a recording artist. Pete, was somewhere in the crowd tonight. The Troubadour on Santa Monica boulevard right between Hollywood and Beverly Hills always had a crowd when Chuck performed. Everyone loved him. He not only sang good. He had an exceptionally great personality. When asked where he got his singing talent. He would always say it was handed down from his grandfather.

After doing an hour and a half show, Chuck took a half hour break and came back on for a second show. They had again filled up the club with waiting guest. While in the dressing room, Pete came in to see him. He told him to come by the studio at his convenience and they would make arrangements to start doing some recording.

All looked well for Chuck. Aside from being a box office draw actor. He was now on his way to becoming a recording artist.

Hollywood, California, Sunday morning February 20th, 1988.

It was a dismal day as Chuck and Susie had breakfast in Susie's apartment. After last nights show at the Troubadour. They had gone out to a favorite spot with some friends for a light snack.

Then to Susie's apartment, and to bed, for some much needed rest.

During breakfast they discussed the letter Chuck had received Friday from Bubba Plunk. Bubba wished them both well and expressed his regrets that he had been so long in writing. The importance of the letter was that he wanted to see if Chuck might could come to Heaven to attend to some business which was beyond his capacity.

The letter continued; "The field as far as the eye can see from the house toward and by town is again full of soybeans—a really beautiful sight.

They are this week starting to harvest. A new soybean oil mill has been built about fifteen miles up the road toward Camden and the whole countryside has been either leased or bought and planted in soybeans. The trailer house community across the highway is all gone, replaced by beans.

The company called, THE OUACHITA OIL MILL, wants to buy your land and extend it out to the highway, doing away with the house and trees and freeing it up to plant more soybeans. I told them you more than likely didn't want to sell. What with the school teacher living there—and, well you know—yer grandpa's spirit more than likely with her. I didn't tell 'em all of that, you know. I just told'em you probably didn't want to sell. But they insist on talking to you. I wouldn't give'em your telephone number. I realize this could be taken care of by telephone Chuck, but there are a couple more personal things too, which you need to help us with. Oscar said to tell you hey—and Chuck, when you come. Come in the daytime. Don't come to Heaven at night."

Chuck sat at the table for quite some time contemplating the letter. He could call Oscar, he thought, but then Bubba seemed to really want him to come. He knew Susie's soap-opera would not be shooting for the next three weeks, maybe she could go with him. He looked up from the letter, she wasn't there. He got up and went into the bedroom. Susie was out on her small overhang patio. She sat on a wicker stool, brushing her shining waist length black hair, pulled over the front of her shoulders.

"Susie, would you like to go to Heaven with me?" asked Chuck.

"Can't. I have to work."

"You're not shooting for three weeks."

"That doesn't mean I can get off. They're re-vamping the whole show. Taking it in a different direction or updating it as the producer says. All the cast have to be there. I'm not so sure I would go anyway with the chance of ol'Charlie's spirit being there—as Bubba mentioned in the letter. And don't you dare bring him back here with you again. I'm having feelings of having experienced all of this before. It makes my skin crawl."

"It makes your skin crawl, huh? What does it smell like when your ass passes your nose?"

"Apple pie Damn-it! Chuck, that's not funny." she said, as she slung the hairbrush at him.

"I know, baby." he put his arms around her and hugged her. "I just couldn't pass it up." he handed her the brush. "I'll go do the dishes."

Susie closed the sliding glass door to the patio, put the brush on the vanity and went into the kitchen with Chuck. They began to clear the table. Susie rinsed the dishes and put them in the dishwasher.

"When are you leaving?" she asked.

"I haven't said I was going yet."

"But I know you are and I certainly can't blame you. If Bubba is in some kind of trouble, as the letter indicated, you need to go right away."

Chuck embraced her and kissed her tenderly. Feeling a special gratification that Susie understood the benevolent brotherhood that existed between Bubba and himself.

"I love you." he said tenderly. "Will you call the airport and get me a flight for this afternoon. I'll go to my apartment and pack a bag—oh, and sometime in the morning, call my agent and tell her I'll be gone for a little while."

"A flight to where?"

"Shreveport, Louisiana."

"Do you want round trip?"

"No, I want know how long I'll be, until I know what's going on."

"You call me as soon as you know what's happening." she said.

Chuck kissed her again and went out the door. She sit down at the table and tried hard to hold back the tears. She knew it couldn't be anything good.

Thoughts from the past raced through her mind. The evilness of the town people trying to kill Chuck. Him killing a deputy sheriff. The rampaging wild hogs, controlled by a grotesque demon from hell. The school teacher trying to kill him. Finding his grandfather dead in a well. Killing the big hog on the stairs. His grandfathers spirit entering him, and coming home with him. And raping me. And, and she began to cry.

Susie drove Chuck out to LAX for his 5 p.m. flight to Shreveport via Delta. He had returned to her apartment before noon. They had about four hours before leaving for the airport. And they didn't talk anymore about Bubba or Heaven.

They took advantage of the time to make love and have sex. She had to awaken him in time to shower and get ready to go. Nothing was said on the way to the airport except for her telling him to be careful and not to forget to call her.

All the way to Dallas, Chuck's mind raced through the past events. Like Susie's did at the apartment. He went through his entire experience in Heaven, starting with his meeting Rose and Spider Webb. He didn't have but the one encounter with them but he thought about them a lot. He always felt that Spider was the greatest character he had ever met. He thought a lot about Argus and the restaurant and his daughter June Ann. He liked Argus and felt very badly about June Ann's demise and Argus having to be sent away. He felt that sick feeling again when he thought about the killing of Elroy out on the highway and hiding out in the woods and meeting Booger Jim and the hogs, God, they were awful, those large packs of rampaging hogs. And Connie, the school teacher, trying to find grandfathers will, he remembered following her across the big field, watching her enticing young ass oscillate in her tight jeans. A shame he thought—that she had to die, buried with grandfather in an old water well. Most of all he remembered being host to grandfather's spirit and he leading him and Bubba through the swamp in the half-track to kill the demon from hell with a flame thrower.

Chuck tried to put it all out of his mind and get some sleep. As soon as he managed to fall asleep the flight attendant announced for everyone to put on their seat belts for entrance to Dallas-Fort Worth International Airport. There was a two hour layover. Chuck had a cinnamon role and coffee, and watched the people before boarding another plane for Shreveport. It was just a short jump over to Shreveport where he rented a car and headed to El Dorado. He figured it would be about time for breakfast when he reached El Dorado. He would then rent a room and eat.

The sun was just showing signs of rising when Chuck rented the room at the Kings Inn and went into the restaurant for a light breakfast. Not seeing anyone he remembered, he went back to his room and stretched out across the bed where he slept soundly for about four hours.

Upon awakening Chuck unpacked his bag and hung two pair of jeans and three shirts in the closet. Put extra underwear and socks in a drawer, went into the bathroom, took a shower, brushed his hair, put on a clean white shirt and headed for Heaven.

On the way, his thoughts drifted back to Pete Andrews, and he hoped he could wind up the business here quite rapidly. While he did not have a movie to start on right away. It would be a good time to start doing some recording. All the way to the Heaven turnoff he day-dreamed about going on the road doing concerts to promote his first album. He thought about how he would have to juggle his time between that and working on motion picture productions. But then, he had always kind of burned the candle at both ends, so to speak. This would be like both ends and the middle too. He did not worry about it. On the contrary, he was delighted to have the conquest to look forward to—he knew he would work it out somehow. He just needed to speed things up here and get back to Hollywood.

Chapter 2

Old memories were renewed rapidly, as the first thing Chuck saw after the population reduction sign, was the clearing where Spider Webb's pork business had been. Chuck pulled over and stopped, remembering his first time here. He thought of the Sheriff and Deputy as they watched him come out of the building and leave.

Chuck continued into town, passed the church, the cemetery and some old antebellum homes before he came to the town hall and Sheriff's office. He saw some cars parked out front and decided to stop and see Oscar before going on down to Bubba's car lot. Oscar and Bubba saw him through the window as he walked up the walk and met him twenty feet from the door.

They ran gleefully from the building with outstretched arms, grabbed and hugged him while talking a mile a minute—mostly incoherent.

"Let's go inside, I have fresh coffee made." said Oscar, enthusiastically.

"You see, Oscar, I told'ya he'd come." Bubba said. "I told'ya!"

Inside the Sheriff's office, Oscar insisted that Chuck sit at his desk. He then poured a cup of coffee and set it on the desk.

"You want cream and sugar?" he asked.

"No thanks, Oscar. I drink it black. Now, before anything else, I want to know if the fire has gone out."

"Not yet." Oscar said. "But it's gone down. That hole has opened up to be quite a large crater. The fire is maybe twenty feet high and they say the crater is about a hundred feet wide. The experts say it will burn out in a few more years and fill with ocean water from underground streams connecting to the gulf of Mexico. Like one did bout sixty-five years ago down in Alto, Louisiana. It has salty gulf water in it and rises and falls with the tide."

Chuck could not help but notice how Bubba was sitting back in his chair looking somewhat apprehensive and perpetually glancing at Oscar.

"Alright guys, spill it, what's the problem?"

Bubba stammered. Oscar interrupted and blurted it out.

"We've got us some vampires!"

Chuck looked at him vacuously for a long period of time.

"VAMPIRES—the word exploded like a tempestuous scream as all the old scary vampire

movies, names and appurtenances raced through and jumbled his mind.

"Count Dracula"

"Bram Stoker"

"Bela Lugosi"

"Wooden Stakes"

"Silver Crucifixus"

"Black Capes"

"Fangs"

"Neck Biting puncturing the jugular vein"

"Drinking blood"

"DRINKING   BLOOD?!!!!—Good   God Almighty!!" Oscar did say vampires—maybe I misunderstood him—No, that was what he said I think."

"Oscar, you did say vampires—didn't you?"

"Yeah—vampires."

Chuck's mind continued to race a mile a minute on things pertaining to vampires. With his elbows on the desk and his forehead in his hands, he sat there for a good hour in silence.

Oscar and Bubba left him alone and walked outside.

"Maybe we were to quick in telling him about the vampires." said Oscar.

"Naugh." Bubba said. "I think he's asleep. Probably just worn out from the trip."

"Ya'think we should wake him and make'em lie down on yer bed?"

"Naugh, let's just let'em sleep. He looks comfortable."

"Ya'know, Bubba." Oscar said. "I'm sure glad Chuck is here. I bet ya'now, we'll git something done bout them vampires."

"Yeah, Chuck will figure something out. I told'ya he'd come."

They both, with justifiable reasoning, thought very highly of Chuck's abilities. They remembered how he put his plan into action to destroy the demon from hell and eradicate Heaven of the grotesque evil swine. They may have forgotten that his grandfather's spirit was leading him in that endeavor. But be as it may, they knew if anyone could get rid of the vampires—it was him. And why not. He's the <u>demon</u> <u>killer</u>. Why not also be the <u>vampire</u> <u>slayer</u>.

Chuck poured the cold coffee out in the restroom, splashed some cold water on his face and went back to the office. *"So much for getting back to Hollywood right away."* he thought. He poured himself some more coffee, sit down and was taking a sip when Oscar and Bubba came in.

"How long have you had these vampires?" he asked.

"They've been here going on to bout six months now. That bout right Oscar?"

"Yeah, Bubba. I'd say bout six months."

"I guess you've seen these vampires?" asked Chuck.

"Yeah, we've seen 'em." Bubba said. "They only come out at night, or on an overcast day. Some of 'em flew down here and looked through the windows two or three times, but Oscar shined a big hand held halogen light on 'em and they flew away."

"They flew?" Chuck asked. "You mean they have wings?"

"Yeah, they were young naked women with wings." Bubba said. "But Oscar ran 'em away with his light. One of 'em stole a woman's baby bout two months ago. She had been to El Dorado to do some shoppin' and got home after sundown. She left the baby in the car seat while she took some packages in the house. When she came out to get her baby she saw one of them flyin' away with it. That about the way it happened Oscar?"

"Yeah, that's bout it. Her husband came home from work and found her by the car screaming. He worked at the oil mill and always got home bout dark. They're colored folks. A number of 'em living in town what works up at the oil mill. They stayed at home all night with their windows boarded up, like everybody in town does. The next morning after sun up they got in the car and came to see me. They were in such a state of shock, especially her, I took'em to the hospital in El Dorado. I was really worried bout her. She went through therapy for bout six weeks. She's back home now. I went to see bout her a couple of days ago. She just sits in the house all the time, reading her bible."

"Is that why all the windows in here, except the two by the door, are all boarded up?" asked Chuck.

"Yeah." answered Oscar. "We didn't want to have to contend with them at more than them two windows. That light has a heavy battery and is hard to lug around real fast."

"Where's your family Bubba. And your wife, Oscar?"

"My wife and kids are staying in El Dorado with her mother." Bubba said. "You know, like before when you were here, and the hogs got so bad. I don't want to put them in any danger."

"I guess them boys are getting big now." said Chuck in politeness. "What about your wife Oscar? Where's she?"

"She just went home a couple of hours ago. She'll be coming back in awhile. And Jim Bob

Barlow—he'll be coming back too. He went to El Dorado to get some shotgun shells."

"Jim Bob is our Mayor, Bubba said. He's making some silver buckshot. He thinks maybe it might kill them. We all went over to Viola Ledbetter's house and gathered up some of her silver from the dining room and Jim Bob melted it down into buckshot. He's made a regular workshop out of his office next door. That's where he's been working on it. He's go'na put garlic in the shells too, right along with the buckshot.What do'ya think Chuck—think it'll work?"

"I really don't know. Guess it's worth a try. I always thought you drove wooden stakes through their heart while they slept—you know, like in the movies."

"Jim Bob said that was just for the movies. He said the best thing would be to get'em into the sunlight. He said that would kill'em for sure, but maybe the silver would do it too."

"We've all been staying here at night." Oscar said. "We figured maybe there's safety in numbers, or something like that. Me and Sandy put up us a bed down the hall in the conference room where the council meets. Jim Bob sleeps on the couch in his office, when he sleeps. He's up all hours working on melting silver, crushing garlic and loading twelve gauge shotgun shells. Oh, and melting wax to use for wadding in the shells. He also has about half a dozen twelve gauge pump shotguns too. Man, that big cherry wood desk in there looks like a bench in a chemistry laboratory. I think his door is open, come on, take a look at it."

As they all started into the hall, Oscar motioned back into the Sheriff's office.

"That twin bed over there in the corner is where Bubba sleeps. We have the windows in our houses all boarded up too."

They made a quick left into the Mayor's office. Oscar didn't like coming into this room because he always thought of Mayor Carl Kelly blowing his brains out while sitting at that big desk. The wild hogs were on a rampage that day, and from a window in the Sheriff's office, Oscar witnessed Sheriff Harley Dobson succumb to the jaws of death. Mayor Kelly, who had a secret (at least he thought it was secret) sexual infatuation for Sheriff Dobson, also saw him rendered and eaten. He turned from the window, sat down behind his desk, removed a pistol from the drawer, cocked it, put the short barrel in his mouth, ran his tongue around it, fancied for a brief moment it was Harley and then he blew the back of his head off.

Chuck looked around the room. The window was boarded up and everything was as Oscar had explained. Except, he wondered about the pasteboard box on the floor next to the chair. It was full of empty shotgun shells. Chuck thought only briefly, "*Do the people in this town still live with covetousness and adulterous sins like I was told of, yes….and WITNESSED when I was here before….Is the evil still here. If Oscar went to Jim Bob's house, would he find Sandy's car there…If not, why did he lie about having to go to El Dorado.*"

If Oscar even suspected, he would not go. He would not want to know. Sandy is his rock, she is his shoulder to lean on. He would overlook any infidelity to keep her. He especially would not go looking for one. They went back into the Sheriff's office. Oscar sit down in a chair in front of his desk while Chuck poured himself another cup of coffee. Bubba leaned back on his bed.

"Hey guys." Chuck asked. "Have you ever wondered why Heaven has these kind of problems and why there seems to be an unknown force of evil always hanging over the town. I know both of you, living here all the time, must have witnessed a lot of deplorable, or depraved, things going on. Like, for example, where did the demon that we killed come from. It's like there's a gate opened from hell and it effects the whole town. Have you ever felt that you may be caught up in the horrible oppressiveness of the town. I sometime have an inkling of it and I only lived here six years."

"I've had my moments." Oscar said. "Back when I was Deputy, I saw a lot of evil. I don't think they knew they were evil though, but they sure knew they were bad. It's always been a bad town."

"Well," Bubba said. "I wasn't born here like ya'll was, but I've seen my share of downright evil doings in this town. I bought my house and car lot property here because it was dirt cheap. I've liked it here and have done well with my business, but like Oscar, I've seen a lot of wicked people here, and I've had my moments of thinking I was one of them. You know, about that gate to hell. There's an old story about a lot of people being burned alive in an old school house on the piece of ground that we call the fairground. Grass has never grown on it and people say that it is evil. Do ya'think it might be that gate to hell?"

"Yeah, Oscar said, I've heard the story bout when they had a beer bash there and wanted yer'grandpaw to pick and sing fer'em and he wouldn't do it because it was at the fairground. He refused to go near the place."

"I've heard that story too." said Chuck, with a pang of sorrow. He had discovered that his parents were killed during that particular beer bash by a bunch of wild hogs.

The three of them would never know how close to the truth they were. If only they had Nathan Ledbetter's chronicle written December 20th, 1911, then they would know.

They would know the horrible truth of how evil can grasp and wrench a man's soul, striping him of all morality. Distorting his mind and views on life and leaving him incorrigibly mad. Nathan Ledbetter had become such a man before relinquishing his last breath of a self induced insanity to the newly arrived demon from hell, deep in the vast swamp bottom to the north of Heaven.

Shortly after Nathan had taken part in the burning of the schoolhouse which terminated the lives of twenty-six innocent people, the demon from hell appeared and set up his kingdom in the swamp bottom. The demon took control of the wild swine and ordered them to host all spirits of the evil people of Heaven as they became available. And so, the unknown evil of the swamp prevailed and continued to grow for years to come. In the stillness of late evenings the people could hear eerie far away sounds emitting from the swamp bottom. These indistinct sounds became a way of life that gave them a lasting sense of insecurity. No one spoke of them because no one understood them. And they feared what they didn't understand.

Chapter 3

Three year old Chucky Abbott slept soundly in his goose-down bed during the biggest ice storm of the century, as Viola Ledbetter, Nathan's ninety some-odd year old daughter, only five miles to the east, sat by her fireplace scrutinizing every morbid detail of her father's chronicle as she burned it page by page.

If Chuck, Bubba and Oscar only had these few excerpts from the chronicle, then they would understand ... *I cannot begin to express the magnitude of terror I feel for this town, yet I cannot escape ... Something will not let me leave, and I fear it might be the evil in MY soul ... The deep acknowledgement of my eternal damnation, that makes me linger among these people who have come to be my family .... What evil is here? ... It is not the people. The people of the town are among the most God fearing I have every known. They never miss a Sabbath service ... not one. No, they are not the ones who have laid the evil down. They, as, I, are enslaved by it ... But do not realize God has cursed the land they dwell on. Everyday they walk with the devil, but still fall to their knees and give praise in the name of Christ ... all the blasphemers ... without a clue as to why they suffer their secret desires. Why their lusts and adulterous sins are so out of their control ...... As evil or dark as they must be. I say it is the land ... cursed by God.*

Winter had come, much like today, thirteen years ago, and something dreadful happened. I dare only to call it dreadful within these pages, for outside of this book, I look upon the occurrence in a different manner, and feel differently, likewise..........

The war with Spain had ended and the soldiers had returned. Only seven men had gone from Heaven ... Six of them returned, three of whom brought back a highly contagious disease and within two weeks we had twenty-six men, women and children suffering, feverish and vomiting, inside the four room school house which was being used as an emergency medical building.

There was a town meeting. A unanimous decision was made to do something to stop the spreading infection. Four men were elected to do the job ... and we did it. David Abbott, Samual Brothers, Zachary Platt and myself barred the doors and burned the school house to the ground. Inside, twenty-six people screamed as their flesh sizzled from their bones and their lives terminated in seconds.

The night was alight from the fire. The whole town watched it burn ... We watched with no remorse ... no regrets. We watched the pustular disease rise into the air, carried by the smoke, and disappear into the sky ... Gone from Heaven forever ...

I told myself that it was the right thing to do. And I still believe that. We did it to spare those poor souls the agony of a slow and profound death. We did what HAD to be done.

But still I wonder about the nature of our actions. Did we do it because we felt we had to, or because we WANTED to? While the building burned, a grin crept across my face which I could not control, and a marvelous joy overwhelmed me. Not that I have the right to call it joy ... It would be better described as an EVIL LUNACY. I wondered if the others might think me mad, but on observing them, I saw that they too were enveloped with smiles and lunacy.

A few years prior to ridding the town of the small-pox epidemic, I became a rich man, I have everything that I could possibly need for the rest of my life. I settled ... built my home here ... and will stay here.

The past week has been one of tragedy. My wife gave birth to a daughter whom we shall call Viola after my own mother. I curse God for not giving me a son.

What evil is here? Before I have written that it is a curse from God. But now I ponder the matter of such a curse. Would a merciful God have his children controlled by evil? No, I think not. The nature of the curse stems not from God ... God has forsaken the people of Heaven ... Such a curse is the work of the devil ... And the devil IS here in Heaven.

Viola Ledbetter had never known her father. He had disappeared when she was a baby.

But now she knew, as she read her bible, cried and prayed. She knew without a doubt in her mind, as she read the scripture over and over.

For I the Lord thy God am a jealous God, visiting the iniquity of the fathers upon the children unto the third and fourth generation of them that hate me;

She knew why she had suffered her life with the unrelenting fate of an abnormal and deplorable affliction.

The town had grown. The population more than tripled since Nathan Ledbetter wrote his chronicle. But the people relatively stayed the same. The wanton immorality, larceny and covetousness remained, as though Heaven were

a breeding ground for evil. And then, COME
THE SWINE.

Jim Bob came in and Chuck noticed that he
didn't bring anything in with him. He shook his
hand and exchanged pleasantries. He reminded
Chuck somewhat of Sheriff Harley Dobson,
ruggedly handsome and physically sound. Bubba
told Jim Bob that Chuck had come to help them
destroy the vampires.

"You know anything about vampires?" Jim
Bob asked Chuck.

"Only what I've seen in the movies." answered
Chuck.

"Yeah, mc too." Jim Bob said. "I'm in hopes
that silver will kill'em.

They say it will kill werewolves, maybe it will
kill vampires too."

"I sure hope so." Chuck said. "Listen, ya'll hold
the fort down and I'll see you in the morning if
the sun is shinning. I have a room in El Dorado
and I'm going there for the night."

"I'll walk out with'ya." said Bubba.

They went out the door and to Chuck's rental
car. Bubba hugged Chuck tight while patting his
back.

"I sure appreciate you coming Chuck. I just hope I ain't got you into something over yer head."

"Don't worry about it partner. Tomorrow we'll go see the soybean man. And then worry about the vampires."

Chuck gave Bubba a reassuring hug and ask him if he wanted to go to El Dorado with him for the night and have a good supper. He told him no. Sandy always cooked them some supper and she would be here with it before sundown.

Chuck left mentally kicking himself for having nefarious thoughts about Sandy. He resolved to quit jumping to conclusions as he drove out of town.

But then, he could not help but remember how this town did things to it's people. The adultery, the covetousness, most he only heard of, some he witnessed, like Connie McGuire (such a waist) and June Ann, yes, and her daddy, Argus. Chuck was confused, he could not help having wicked thoughts when the evidence was laid out in front of him. Especially here in Heaven. "MY GOD." he said half aloud to himself. "Could it be." Could it be that I'm just as evil and corrupt as any one of them. I AM a part of Heaven. My roots are here. I belong to this town. I was born here and lived here for six years. Doesn't that qualify me as being a legitimate resident with equal rights to the same lunacy and immorality as the rest of the people of Heaven. Have I been hiding from myself? I know damn well there's something amiss with Jim Bob and Sandy. How do I see and know these things if I'm not a true Heavenite.

Chuck parked in front of his room at the King's Inn and went inside. He washed his face and stared at himself for a good long time in the mirror. He wondered if he might could see into his mind and possibly rectify the problem of why he felt so differently when he was in Heaven than he did at home in Hollywood. Could it be that in the recesses of his mind he knew that Heaven was truly his real home. He washed his face again, brushed his hair and went to the restaurant. He had to wait a little while. The King's Inn always had good food and was usually crowded at dinner time. In a bit he was seated and asked if he wished to go through the buffet or order. He decided on the buffet. About half way through his dinner a young lady came to his table and asked for his autograph. He had noticed them earlier looking at him and whispering. He graciously signed her paper and thanked her. It still always gave him a good feeling to sign an autograph. When he went to pay his check the cashier called him by name and told him they were pleased to have him back again. "It's been three years." he said. "I'm amazed you remembered me." She told him that she had seen him in a lot of movies and she expressly liked the one where he played the country singer.

"You did do the actual singing in that movie. Didn't you?"

"Yes, I did."

"I told'em it was you. Somebody said it was dubbed. I told'em it was really you."

"Well, you were right. It was really me."

She said all of the employees watched for his movies. He had become a living legend at the King's Inn. She asked him about a picture to put on the wall. He said he would most definitely send one when he returned to Hollywood.

Chuck showered and went to bed early. All night he tossed and tumbled and dreamed of vampires. Old vampires, young vampires and yes, flying vampires, young naked female flying vampires. He awakened early out of a nightmarish dream about a young naked vampire with wings trying to seduce him. She made no attempt to bite him. She held him down with her wings fluttering above them while she tried to remove his jeans. She was so strong as she straddled his legs and tried to get his jeans down that he was helpless to resist. Had she gotten them down before giving up and flying away, he was so frightened he could have never performed anyway. He awoke in a cold sweat and went straight to the shower trying to erase the dream from his mind.

After showering he found a fluff of down on his bed. Like from the inner growth of a birds feathers. He examined it and wondered. Where? How?

"No!"he said aloud. It was only a dream. A hallucination. "I'm not going to get into this bullshit of trying to read reality into a simple dream" he said aloud to himself. "Now, I'm talking to myself—Shit."

Chuck dressed, brushed his hair, and headed back to Heaven. He and Bubba were supposed to do something this morning. "What?" He assumed that he would think of it by the time he got there. As assumptions go. It immediately popped into his brain. They were to go see the soybean man about the property. Then he will see the school teacher and let her know he is not selling the house. After that, he figured to look around some. Go by the cemetery and go see if Booger Jim was still alive. *"Probably is."* he thought. Three years is nothing to him. *"He probably passed a hundred long ago. If nobody bothers him. He'll live forever. The old man's crazy as a Bessie bug anyway."* Chuck could almost hear him. *"Ya'think's Booger Jim's crazy—don't'cha!"* Yeah, I've got to go see him. He might know something about the vampires. He knew all about haints and hob-gobblins.

Chapter 4

Bubba had told Chuck in the letter about the sophisticated school teacher that leased the house and wanted to stay even after they closed the school and started busing the kids to El Dorado. They turned off the highway and drove toward the old home place. Bubba had described her as being in her mid to late thirties, pretty, discreet, and occasionally somewhat egoistical. He noticed the pecans all over the ground which had never been picked up as they drove up to the front of the house and the lady came out on the porch. She was a beautiful lady, mid thirties, displaying an air of dignity.

"Oh, I forgot to tell you, she has a bit of an accent. I don't know where she's from, but her lease is paid up through another seven years."

Chuck and Bubba got out of the car and went up to the steps. The lady looked concerned. She stood in front of the screen door which lead into the living room.

"Hello, my name is Chuck Abbott. This here is Bubba Plunk. You've met him."

"Yes." she said.

"Chuck is the one what owns the property." said Bubba.

"So?" she answered. "Is your visit about the man that wants to buy the house?"

"No Mam, You can rest assured that I'm not selling the house. I was just in town and thought I'd drop by and see how everything was and if you needed anything."

"Everything is fine. I don't need anything." she said in a relieved tone.

"Mam." Bubba asked. "Would you mind if I picked up some of these pecans?" he motioned toward the pecan trees.

"Go ahead." she said pleasantly. Bubba went into the yard, put a few pecans in his pocket, and continued around the house looking for a container.

Chuck asked the lady where she was from. Without hesitation she answered. "I'm from London, England. *My God—Ahhaa.*" she stammered, weaved uncontrollably, grabbed the sides of her head and pushed on her temples. *Pain—Pain—Excruciating   Pain   Anguish —unbearable Torture.*

Succumbing to the *evil hurt* and falling heavily against the door, she slipped into unconsciousness and lost control to a will much greater than her own. Emitting a dark fog from her mouth. She spoke in a weak raspy male voice.

"Hey, Chucky… what the fuck you doing here boy… I thought I'd never see you again… how the hell you doing?"

"I'm doing just great ol'man." Chuck said. "How about you?"

"I'm fine… I have this lovely bitch here that I have my way with all the time. Sometime I even think she knows it… but she don't let on if she does. Yeah, I'm fine… I get a lot of poontane."

"Is that all she does, is give you poontane?"

"Naugh, she's got some damn blood suckers in the two back bedrooms, she spends a lot of time looking after them."

"Alright grandfather, I've got to go now, but I'll be back again soon."

"Bye Chuckie…come back when you can stay longer… how's that pretty little girl of yer's… you still knockin' the bottom out of that?"

The lady was oblivious to what had transpired. To her the time lapse was but a fleeting moment of excruciating pain. *"An aneurysm"* she thought *"In the back of my head."*

Bubba came around the house as Chuck backed away from the steps. Chuck motioned him to the car and they left as the lady was going into the house rubbing the back of her head. Chuck had noticed the windows were blacked out. He let it pass without giving it much thought. It was only mid- morning and the sun was out in full force. They decided to go to the Ouachita Oil Mill.

Chuck did not tell Bubba, of the incident on the porch. He didn't want Jim Bob or anyone going off half cocked and ruining their chances of destroying the vampires. *"I'll figure out what to do at the proper time."* he thought.

Chuck silently meditated about his grand-father's earthbound spirit. He knew he was evil and cruel, he had known it a long time, probably even demoniac. Could he possibly be the gate they had talked about. Nonetheless, he had demonized that pretty lady and is now living with vampires.

The only thing Bubba said was, hell, I didn't get any pecans.

About fifteen miles up the highway toward Camden, they rounded a curve and drove head on into a different world. The change was so unexpected it extracted a huge gasp from Chuck. Straight ahead in the bite of the curve loomed a vast mill with two huge silos about fifty feet wide and eighty feet tall. Just past the silos was the office complex sitting back from the highway with built in truck scales on the far side of it. About six long open bed soybean trucks were waiting to be weighed, the huge two story mill was next in line with a railroad spur track going through the building with three round liquid cars waiting to go through.

They drove on past the complex while looking it over and then turned around and went back to the parking lot in front of the offices. They sat there for awhile feeling dwarfed by the tall silos.

"Bubba, do you know anything about oil mills?"

"There was one just like this where I lived in Louisiana before I came to Heaven, except it also processed cottonseed."

"Do you know exactly what their purpose is. Give me a rundown."

"Well, they extract the oil from the soybeans. The oil has a lot of purposes, but mainly it's used for cooking oil. Hell, you can buy it in any grocery store. Then they take the meal what's left, dry it, add some blackstrap molasses to it and sack it up for cattle feed. They make pellets with the same mixture. It goes through a heated compression cylinder and comes out breaking off about one inch in diameter and three inches long. They sell them for cattle feed too. A lot of people, like me, use to buy them in hundred pound sacks and weight'em down with cinder blocks to bait fishing holes. They ship out the oil and cattle feed on a big scale. You see them big round pipes slanted down from the top of the silos. They go to where the trucks are unloaded by a large vacuum into a pit where a big auger inside of them takes the beans up and empties them into the silos.

Another auger at the bottom takes the beans to the cooker as needed."

Chuck looked at Bubba in absolute amazement.

"Damn, Bubba. You're not near as dumb as you make out to be."

Bubba grinned from ear to ear, taking it as a complement.

They got out of the car and started across the parking lot toward the front of the office complex which was nestled under a large fifty foot high sign which read. OUACHITA OIL MILL.

"Tell me again, Bubba, what is this man's name?"

"Parker—Milton Parker."

Milton Parker was a robust man with square jaws and a friendly smile. He sat at his desk with his shirt sleeves turned up to his elbows and his necktie loosened. He raised up as Chuck and

Bubba were escorted in, reached over the desk to shake their hands and with a big smile told them to have a seat. They sat in the two chairs in front of the desk.

"So you're the young man that owns the Abbott property. And Mister Plunk, how have you been sir?"

"Fine, thank you."

"And Mister Abbott. Mister Plunk said your name is Chuck?" he said in the way of a question.

"Yes sir, my name is Chuck to most everyone. My actual name is Charles Abbott, the third."

"I see—well, I assume you're ready to sell your property. I've taken the liberty of having the papers drawn up. I'm sure they will meet with your approval. We're giving you top dollar for the property."

"Mister Parker sir,—your assumptions are wrong. I came up here to let you know that I have no intentions of selling the property. I will continue to lease you the portion of the property which you now lease. But the home place will remain as is. I'm very absolute about this. I was born there, my father was born there, and my grandfather was born there, as was his father. In fact, my grandfather still resides there." Chuck quit talking, fearing he had said to much. *"Why didn't I tell him, NO, I don't want to sell and let it go at that…. Damn, I guess it's anxiety."* he thought.

"Well, God-damn'it to hell, why did you come up here wasting my time. When you change your mind. Come back and see me then."

Chuck and Bubba got up and left. On the way across the parking lot Bubba grinned freely.

"Man, you sure gave him what for. Guess he won't be hounding me no more bout buying the house."

Driving back to Heaven. Chuck and Bubba watched two combines harvesting and threshing soybeans where the trailer house community once flourished.

"Hey, Bubba. How many crops a year do they get?"

"Two."

"What say let's stop at the café and have a hamburger."

"Yeah, okay." Bubba answered. "If it's open. It don't open much during the day. Seems to do a good business at night though. I think it must be vampires meeting there."

"Well, Damn." Chuck said. "I don't want to go there then.—Argus sure use to serve some good hamburgers there."

"We've got plenty of time." Bubba said. we could go on into El Dorado and eat."

"You want to stop and see if Oscar wants to go?" asked Chuck.

"Sure" Bubba said. "We could get us some thinking done."

"Thinking about what?"

"Vampires—you know—how to get rid of 'em."

Damn, Chuck thought. He had became so enthused in Bubba's lesson about the soybean oil mill and the meeting with Milton Parker, he completely forgot about the vampires. He had no idea what to tell Bubba and Oscar. In fact, he had no idea what to do or where to begin to eradicate Heaven of vampires. The only thing in his favor was that now he knew where some dwelled. In his own house with his grandfather's spirit.

"*What to do?*"

"*What to tell Bubba and Oscar?*"

"*I can't let them down... I must think of something*"

"*Damn, Chuck... settle down... don't lose it*"

"*Just play it by ear, Man... Something will come to you...*

"*Remember......you're the demon killer.....*

Oscar was alone and jumped at the chance to get out for awhile. "Where ya'll want to go eat at." he asked. "Ya'know the Town House is real good, they have a good home cooking kind of buffet there."

"I kind of thought about going to the King's Inn where I'm staying." Chuck said. "Tell you what. Let's vote on it."

"I'd like the King's Inn." said Bubba.

"I guess I'm with ya'll." said Oscar.

"Then it's unanimous." Chuck said. "Good choice Oscar." Oscar scratched his head and looked somewhat befuddled.

On the way to the King's Inn Chuck told them about his dream. Although, as he was known to do on occasion, he added a lot of juicy tidbits to the story. He did not mention the fact that he was to scared out of his wits to perform. He just told them he couldn't bring himself to do it.

"Well, shitfire." Bubba said. "Whyn't you go ahead and fuck'er?"

"Bubba." Oscar said. "Ya'know that would be what they call infidelity and you know Chuck ain't that way."

Chapter 5

The phone rang only twice at Blake's world renowned antiquities dealership in New York. Mister Stanley Blake Junior answered.

"Hello, Blake's Antiquities. How may I help you."

"Hello, my name is Victor Boc." came a strong and articulate voice. "I am calling from Cluj Napoca, Romania. I would like to know if you would be interested in buying some tapestries."

"What kind of tapestries do you have Mister Boc?"

"Yes, you need to know that—I have eight tapestries—thirty feet wide by forty feet high. They are lavender with battle scenes woven into them from the X11[th] century wars."

"Good Lord." Blake exclaimed as he stood up. "Are they in good condition?" "Where can I see them?"

"Yes, they are in excellent condition. They have hung in my ancestral castle since it was built in the mid thirteen hundreds. I am told they are priceless. But I would like to hear an offer."

"When would be a good time to see them?"

"Anytime Sir. I'm always home."

"I'll have one of my people to come right away. Give me directions."

"Fly into Clug-Napoca. It's the largest city in Romania. I believe it is now near three hundred fifty thousand. Plenty of places to find lodging. Hire a car to the Boc-Bella Castle. Everyone know where it is—eleven miles out of town."

"Alright, Mister Boc. Someone will be there soon."

"Thanks. I'll be waiting."

Victor hung up the telephone. He had dropped BELLA, the second half of the family name hundreds of years ago, but the castle remained known as, Boc-Bella.

Victor had no intentions of selling his tapestries. He was wanting to talk to someone who had the mental capabilities of being a guardian or trustee, someone who could effectively function as a KEEPER. He knew that a buyer from Blake's would be knowledgeable in invoices, licenses, crating and shipping. All he had to do now was talk him into it.

He awaited the man from Blake's with an anxious anticipation. He wanted so much, after eleven hundred years, to take a vacation away from the castle, cross the ocean and see the new world he had heard so much about. In his limited alliance with Satan he had learned of enormously wicked and evil places in the United States where there were open gates from hell. Where he would fit in without being in much danger of being unwelcome. There is such a place in the Region of Massachusetts. Another in the Region of New Mexico. And one in the Region of Arkansas, ironically called Heaven. A depraved grin crept across his face as he thought about living in Heaven, be it none the less in the region of Arkansas.

Stanley Blake Junior wasted no time in calling one of his most efficient buyers. Elizabeth Day in London England. Actually, Elizabeth maintained her office in London and lived to the east in Oxford. She had it fixed so her London telephone would ring in her Oxford home. She took all the information from Mister Blake and told him she would get right on it.

Elizabeth, originally from Moline, Kansas, fell in love with Oxford when she attended Oxford University where she received a Roades scholarship. She had stayed and made Oxford her home. Since, she had traveled worldwide examining and buying for Blake's Antiquities.

Forty eight hours after receiving the call from Stanley Blake, Elizabeth Day banged the heavy knocker on the huge wooden door at the Boc-Bella Castle. Momentarily, a tall thin pale man with a pronounced overbite and two protruding buck teeth opened the door and looked at her. He looked exactly like the vampires from the old movies. Knowing well that she was in the center of the Transylvania Region, She felt a slight shiver down her spine.

"I'm from Blake's Antiquities in New York. I'm here to see the tapestries. Are you Mister Boc?" she asked feebly.

"No, I'm the butler." he said. "My name is Alex. Come into the parlor and I'll get Master Boc."

"Thank you, she said timorously as she stepped through the door." The butler left her in the parlor. She was amazed at the valuable antiques in the room. From suits of armor that looked to be from the X111th century to axes, swords and shields that adorned the walls.

"Hello." Victor Boc said as he entered the room and extended his hand.

"I'm Victor Boc. Alex said you are from Blake's. Forgive me if I'm somewhat taken aback. I was expecting a man."

"I'm sorry if I disappointed you Mister Boc."

"Oh, no, no. Forgive me, I'm not disappointed at all. I'm sure you will do just fine. Come into the sitting room and see the tapestries. Could I offer you some tea?" He motioned to Alex for the tea.

Elizabeth was amazed to see such a handsome young man in his late twenties. She too, was taken aback, as she expected to see a much older man. She followed him through the vestibule into an adjoining room. It was a large room with tapestries hanging around the entire room from the forty foot ceiling. In the center of the room were four large couches placed in a square facing inward. Aside from the couches the room was empty.

Elizabeth was captivated and lost in the beauty and enchantment of the tapestries. As the awe and fascination enveloped her, Victor sat on one of the X11th century Florentine couches and watched her with a suppressed secret admiration.

After quite some time of looking at all the intricate battle scenes woven into the tapestries, Elizabeth sat down on the couch across from Victor, facing him. Victor placed his hand over his mouth as he uttered a yawn.

"Please forgive me, Miss Day. It is Miss, is it not?"

"Yes, it is."

"I'm very sorry about the yawning. I'm not accustomed to being up this time of day. I'm more of a nocturnal person."

"Mister Boc, I'm absolutely astounded at the beauty and perfectibility." she stammered over the word, "of the workmanship. I am at a loss as to even venture a guess as to an offer."

"Yes, I know. I told Mister Blake over the telephone that they were priceless. Miss Day, may I call you Elizabeth?"

"Please do."

"Yes, Elizabeth—that's a beautiful name. Tell me, have you ever given any thought to the possibilities of living forever?" Surprised by such a question, she readily answered.

"No, not really."

"Yes, I suppose one would have to know that they would live well. In the surroundings of elegance and wealth."

She looked at him in a bewildered and confused state of uncertainty.

"Mister Boc. About the tapestries"

"Please. Call me Victor—yes, the tapestries. You know, Elizabeth, I have absolutely no intentions of selling them. They were only a ploy to get you here. I needed to talk to someone of your intellect about going to work for me." As trepidation set in. A nervous dread made her tremble. His talk about living forever and going to work for him. It was confusing. She must regain her composure. She put on a delightful pretentious smile.

"So, Victor. What kind of work do you have in mind?"

"Yes, you do need to know that. It wouldn't be to much different from what you do for Blake's. Making invoices, acquiring licenses, crating and shipping."

"Mister Boc. Victor, I'm very happy with the job I have."

"Yes, I'm sure you are. But I can offer you so much more than Blake can. Please hear me out. I will, how is it said?—cut to the chase. Yes, well first I must tell you not to be alarmed or frightened at what I say. You will be perfectly safe. No harm shall befall you here." Elizabeth looked expressionless at him as he continued to talk.

"Elizabeth, I am a vampire. I was born a vampire over eleven hundred years ago." She cracked a slight disbelieving smile.

"Victor, I don't know if I should scream or laugh. Eleven hundred years old, huh. You don't look a day over nine hundred."

They both forced a feeble and languorous laughter, ending in a stupefied uneasy stare from Elizabeth.

"Yes, I suppose it is hard for one to accept. Not being associated with true vampire realities and traditions. We have been wrongly labeled as being wicked monsters, going around biting everyone we see. Being categorized in that way to make movies and sell books. In reality we are a very passionate, loving and affectionate breed. Not at all the repugnant and abominable creatures that we're made out to be."

Elizabeth had become extremely frightened and was trembling. Victor, was quick to notice. He reassured her that she was in no danger, and in an effort to quell her fear, he continued to tell her how vampires had grossly been misrepresented,

"*Yes.*" he said to himself. "*It's working... I see it in her face and eyes.*"

"Well now, assuming you're not jesting." she said in diffidence. "And I now believe that you're not. Tell me why you would want me to work for you."

"Yes, well—I'm planning to take a short vacation. Maybe three or four years overseas to the New World. There is a place in the region of Arkansas. By name it is called Heaven. I have found it on the Atlas. It is a very small village with larger cities not to far away. You would go in advance and find a place to live. Preferably in the countryside."

"Surely, you're not expecting me to live in the country with you."

"Yes, by all means. With me and my three brides."

"Three brides?" Elizabeth marveled.

"Yes, Spring, Summer and Autumn. My beautiful brides. I have to take them."

"By all means, you have to take Spring, Summer and Autumn. Are these real women, Victor?"

"Yes, they are flesh and blood, the same as you and I. We have been married for over a thousand years. I say the same as you and I, but I must recount that. They have something which we do not. They have wings."

"Wings?"

"Yes, beautiful, shinning black wings."

"Alright, Victor. I've heard about enough without seeing something. Could I possibly meet your brides."

"Yes, of course, if they are not sleeping."

Victor got up and walked around by the end of the couch. "You stay here and I'll bring them to you."

He went through a door at the end of one of the tapestries. Elizabeth awaited his return, perplexed and in wonderment of the excuse he might offer when he returned without his winged wonders, or better yet, his flying brides. From her amusing witticism was borne a sarcastic smile.

"Why" she thought. *"Is this young man playing this kind of charade with me. To what avail? could he really believe he is a vampire? but then he is in the supposedly vampire region of the country. He does live in a castle. And rightly enough, it looks vampirish. I wonder? Could it be?"*

Chapter 6

Elizabeth's disparaging thoughts quickly vanished as Victor returned, followed by his brides. They were drapped in bright thin silk with their wings folded over it. Elizabeth stood as if the Queen of England had entered. *"My God"* she thought. *"They are beautiful… like white porcelain china dolls."* She knew she must sit down. She felt to weak to continue to stand. She quivered, as Victor brought the brides into the square of couches. She knew she must sit down and hoped they would not be insulted.

On the contrary. Much to her relief, they all smiled and sit down. The brides sat sideways on the edge of the couch to compensate for their wings. Victor remained standing.

"Let me introduce everyone. Ladies, this is Miss Elizabeth Day. I'm in great desire of preping her for our friend and keeper during our vacation. So you be nice to her. Elizabeth, my beautiful bride with the long blonde curls is called Spring. Her given name and family name is, Dominique Milosovici Boc-Bella. The Redhead with the hair resembling your Little Orphan Annie is called Summer. Her given name and family name is; Alexandra Dragulescu Boc-Bela. The stunning beauty with the long straight black hair is called Autumn. Her name is Nicolae Nicolescu Boc-Bela. Ladies. You can return to whatever it was you were doing. I'm sure we will all get along fine."

The brides got up and filed by Elizabeth . Each of them leaned over and lovingly kissed her on the cheek. Elizabeth fought hard to keep from succumbing to unsciousness. And then, they were gone, faded away behind a tapestry.

Victor noticed the fright in her eyes. He sat on the couch sideways beside her with his right leg and knee on the couch so as to be facing her. He took her left hand into his.

"Yes, Elizabeth. I know all of this, being so sudden, is extremely hard to accept. I believe you are having a slight anxiety attack. So, I'm just going to explain some of the job descriptions and benefits to you and acquire you a suite at a hotel in town so you can rest and make your decision. I will have Alex to take you there and see that you are settled in. You take your time. If there is anything you might need while you are there, they have all kind of shops in the hotel and a fabulous restaurant—so I am told. Don't resist to buy anything you need, or want. They have clothing shops there too." He glanced at her attire and wondered if she had brought anything else. With the presupposed anticipation of hiring her, he saw that he may have a problem in getting her to dress more elegantly. *"A little finesse may be in order."* he thought. "Cost is of no consequence." he said. "You just charge whatever you need to your suite. And always buy the best and most elegant clothes available." he smiled at her.

Elizabeth probably would never know that the Boc-Bella estate owned the hotel where she would be staying. The estate had purched the hotel when it was built some one hundred years ago, due to the large tourist attraction in the Transylvania Region. Many of the old castles over the years had been opened to tourist, except for the Boc-Bella and a few more which would never be opened to anyone except by personel invitation.

"Yes now, the first thing for you to do, assuming you take the job, is for you to go to London and close your office down, do away with the phone number, after calling and getting out from under Blake. Then you will continue on to the United States, find the place called Heaven in the Arkansas Region, lease or buy a place in the countryside. Now, it must be big enough to accommodate all four of us, with three large bedrooms, two of which are joined. Then, you will see that the windows are blacked out in the entire house. Especially the two adjoining bedrooms. The back of the two adjoined rooms shall have no furniture. The forward of the two rooms will have about four big soft mattresses on the floor, stacked in twos, close together. Then find the very best satin sheets you can and cover the mattresses. Next, find some soft throw pillows, probably about a dozen or eighteen, have them covered with the most exquisite silk and satin you can find. I anticipate you will need to go to a larger city to find the mattresses and linens. Probably the place called Little Rock, it seems to be a large city. The throw pillows can be light and bright in different colors. When all of that is accomplished you will return to Boc-Bella to acquire the proper documents and make arrangements to fly us to the United States in our caskets, under fictitious names for burial. Oh, you will probably have to furnish the rest of the house and your bedroom. Make it nice, remember, cost is no object. If you need a new car or anything personal, don't hesitate to get it. Before you leave Alex will get you some credit cards from the bank. Yes—and now the benefits. For being our keeper and taking good care of us. You will live well and have anything you want. But I must stress that you will have to be dedicated to your job. Now that that has been said. Here is the binder. Being a born vampire. I carry the genes in my blood to give you immortality. Once our vacation is over, you will drink from my blood and live forever. Yes—now Elizabeth, you think it over carefully before you give me your answer. Are you feeling better?"

"Yes, I think I am."

"Yes, good" Victor leaned in and kissed her cheek before standing.

"Alex will be in momentarily and take you to your hotel."

Victor disappeared behind the tapestries. In less than five minutes Alex came in.

"Miss Day, you are ready to go to the hotel." he said in the tone of a question.

"Yes, thank you."

They went out the door where she noticed a black Mercedes Benz in the drive. Alex rushed ahead and opened the passenger door for her. They started down the drive toward the main road.

"Mister Alex Sir. "I left my bag in a locker at the airport."

"Yes, Miss. We shall go get it. Please don't refer to me as Mister or Sir. I am your servant and shall obey your bidding and see to your needs the same as I do for the Master."

"Thanks, Alex. It's also good to have you for a friend."

"I appreciate that Miss. One can never have to many friends. I shall be honored to be your friend."

"Then please call me Elizabeth."

"Thank you Miss Elizabeth." he said with a pleasing smile. "Elizabeth?"

"Yes?"

"Only practicing." he laughed.

Alex and Elizabeth soon stopped at the airport. He went inside the terminal with her and watched her remove her bag from the locker. They then stopped at the bank and she went inside with him in case they may need personal information from her for the credit cards. The banker already had the cards ready. An American Express card for traveling and a Visa card for purchases and cash. They had a no limit face value and the banker needed nothing from her. He laughingly made a statement about seldom ever issuing an American Express card from here as he handed them to Alex. Alex handed them to her to put in her purse. She asked if she could get some cash for walking around money. The banker took her Visa card and ask her how much. A thousand dollars should do, she said. He charged her card and returned it with the cash. She and Alex then went to the hotel. He carried her bag and they went up the elevator to her suite. He put the bag on a table and said if there was nothing else he could do for her, then he would be leaving. She asked him if she should keep receipts for purchases. He told her, "No Miss. You're carte-blanche. The bank will keep up with the sales invoices as they come in. You don't have to try to keep up with them. I'll go now. If you are in need of anything, call me at the Castle. Just tell the operator to ring the Boc-Bella Castle. I'll answer the phone." She thanked him and he left.

Elizabeth was tired. It was now nearing six o'clock in the evening. She went into the bedroom and turned back the covers, took a shower, and got into bed. Everything Victor had told her was racing through her mind as she slipped off to sleep. She awoke early around six a.m. and got up hungry. After slipping on the same clothes she had pulled off and mentally debating calling room service. She changed her mind and went down to the hotel restaurant, ate a hearty breakfast, waited for the Beauty Salon to open, had her hair trimmed and got a facial and a manicure. While being in the restaurant she noticed a lot of people which she later determined to be tourist. She also remembered seeing them when she arrived earlier in the morning. It surprised her that this region of Romania attracted so many tourist. The Ladies clothing store carried an exquisite line of fine apparel. Elizabeth purchased a nice black pant suit, a small hat, a pair of black dress gloves and a white silk scarf. She returned to her room and tried on the pant suit. A perfect fit. All the while she was thinking about what Victor said about the job. She called room service and gave them the pant suit to have the wrinkles pressed out and thought briefly about the immortality that Victor spoke of. Her mind reflected on her life and what might become of her in the future. She remembered her parents and how they became disassociated with her when she had moved to England. She remembered trying to call them numerous times but they would not talk to her. She left the ball in their court, but they never called. After getting out of school and going to work for Blake's, she could never keep a boyfriend for being gone worldwide so much on business. She had no one that would ever miss her unless it was Stanley Blake Junior, and that was all strictly business. Reflecting on getting to old to continue working, and living in an old folks home with no one to ever come see her, was a sorely and piteous image. That's when she made up her mind. With the lure of immortality, as Victor had surmised. Elizabeth decided to take the job. She would make a reservation for a flight to London for tomorrow, stay here another night and call Alex in the morning to let Victor know he had his keeper.

Victor had not told her of his anxiousness to move or of the extenuating circumstances surrounding his anxiousness. He had heard rumors that the local police were going to set up some kind of special task force to try and elimanate the vampires from the castles that would not open up to tourist. He knew that would include Boc-Bela along with a few others. They say these vampires are feeding on tourist and they are going to ruin the tourist trade. So, consequently he decided to move away until this hopefully blowed over, His plans were to have Alex clean up the castle and rid it of any signs of vampires ever being there. Then he could have it opened up to the tourist. Alex was not a vampire, which he could easily prove. But Victor gave him the option of staying there or turning it over to the Tourist Bureau people to show and he moving to the hotel. Which ever he wished.

Victor did not worry but was readily concerned about his Uncle Lestor and other relatives living in Bela Castles scattered throughout the small towns in the mountains to the immediate north. He knew the news had gotten to them and they would do what ever they deemed best. They, as he, had gone through these vampire hunts before with implacable results. There were always options and different ways of mitigating. But this time Victor decided to use it as an excuse to get away for a while. He did, so much want to take a trip. Have an adventure. After all, having never taken a trip. He had been cooped up here for a lot of years.

Chapter 7

Elizabeth had an 11a.m. flight to London the following morning and had gotten her pant suit back from the cleaners. She would call Alex in the morning. After going down and having a light lunch, sitting around being bored all the afternoon, going back down for dinner, sitting around some more, she had a sleepless night. She assumed she must have eaten to much, but in all reality it was the anxiousness of the upcoming events keeping her from sleeping. Morning came early. She was up and dressed by 7 a.m. She went down and ate breakfast. At 8 o'clock she called Boc-Bella and talked to Alex, telling him to let Victor know that he had a keeper and she would be on her way to London at 11 a.m. to get things taken care of there and then on the way to Heaven. Alex told her Victor would be pleased and that he wanted her to get them moved as soon as possible, and he would await, with much anticipation, her arrival back here. "Miss Elizabeth, I know it's going to take a while to get everthing done. But when you do, call and let me know when you're on the way back and I'll start preparing them for the trip."

Elizabeth undressed, laid her new pant suit out on the bed, got clean underware from her bag, put her other clothes in the bag and took a shower. She dressed in her new clothes, put on her new hat and her silk scarf, picked up her bag and purse, looked around the room to see if she had everything and went down to the beauty salon. She had her hair and face re-done, checked out, and got a cab to the airport. She needed to check in an hour early and she was just going to make it. She slept on the airplane.

On arriving in London, she retrieved her car at the airport, went to her office, called and informed Blake that she no longer worked for him due to a chronic incurable illness. She told him the man in Romania had decided not to sell and she was, due to her health, moving back to the United States. He told her that he sorrily regretted losing her and hoped her illness improved soon. She had the telephone disconnected and closed the office. She then drove to Oxford, picked up two suit cases of clothes and personal belongings and closed the house with the intentions of keeping the rent paid. She drove back to the London airport and took the next flight to JFK in New

York with transfer to Little Rock International Airport via DFW in Dallas Texas.

Once she arriving in Little rock she placed her baggage on hold and took a cab to a Lincoln dealership in town where she bought a new black Lincoln town car, purchased an Arkansas map and found her way south to Heaven. She drove around town in short order, seeing no realtors, she went to the Sheriff's office to acquire information. She told Oscar she was looking for a place to lease or buy out in the countryside. He immediately thought of Bubba and Chuck's homeplace. He called Bubba.

Bubba took her to see the house. She looked it over carefully and asked him for a ten year lease which she would pay in it's entirety—in advance. They drove into El Dorado and had the lease drawn up. While there she went to the DMV and acquired an Arkansas drivers license. On returning to Heaven she dropped Bubba off at his truck in front of the Sheriff's office and gave him a hundred dollar tip for keeping him from his work most of the day. He told her that wasn't necessary but he kept it anyway and thanked her. He went home and wrote Chuck a letter of explanation, included her sizeable check in it, and mailed it to him. He told Chuck that she said she was a school teacher. Not knowing the school would be shut down before she had a chance to apply for a position, would be fine with her. She went to the house and made a list of everything she would need for the house. She drove back to El Dorado and rented a room for the night. Next morning early she headed to Little Rock to find what she needed. She was lucky to find most everything in a place called Lowell's. She bought four king size mattresses, two complete sections of styrofoam egg-crate material to cover the two top mattresses and four king size black satin sheets. A new stove and refrigerator equipped with butane jets. She decided that her bedroom which was directly in front of the other two would surface as is, as would the living room across the hallway from her bedroom. She did buy new sheets for her bed and made arrangements for delivery. She gave them directions to the house in Heaven. They told her where there was a large linen store across the street in a mall, where she could probably find the silk throw pillows that she was looking for. She did find them in vibrant bright colors. She picked out two dozen and had them put in the back seat and trunk of her car. She went back to Heaven and put the new sheets on her bed. She found the electricity was on, so she stayed the night there and planned tomorrow to get the black plastic ground covering and tools that she needed to black out the windows over the entire house. She also figured the lights were to bright, so she would get a sixty watt bulb for each room. It was close to dark so she went to bed without supper. She would get up early and have breakfast in El Dorado, accquire her materials and come back to work on the house.

No, she thought, I must first get the furniture out of the two back rooms. So, she called Bubba Plunk and ask him if he could get someone to help him move the furniture to the barn. She said she would make it worth their while. He said they would be there directly. When she hung up, it dawned on her to get the telephone number changed to an unlisted number. When Bubba and the man that worked for him showed up. She showed Bubba what to do and excused herself to go to El Dorado to get the supplies.

The first thing that Elizabeth did in El Dorado was to have breakfast and take care of the telephone. She changed it to her name, and had the unlisted number before leaving the telephone company. She then went to the local Lowell's store and purchased an ample supply of black double layered heavy plastic yard covering. Sissors to cut it and a wall stapler to put it up with. She also bought a vacumn cleaner and dusting material.

A small folding ladder and two gallons of black paint and paint rollers to cover the walls. Some sixty watt light bulbs and a few odds and ends she thought may come in handy. It was noon by the time she got through so she had some lunch and then stopped at a grocery store and bought a twelve pack of cokes, a gallon of milk, a loaf of bread and some lunch meat.

By the time she returned to the house, the Lowell's truck from Little Rock had arrived, Bubba had them to unload everything on the front porch. He and his helper had already taken the old furniture to the barn. They took the new stove and refridgerator in and hooked them up. They then took the old ones to the barn, and stored everything to the side where she could park her car in the barn. Bubba said that was much to nice a car to leave out in the open. She said she could handle the rest, but if she needed him, she would call. She gave them a hundred and fifty dollars each, asking if that would be enough. Way more than enough, Bubba said, as he accepted it. She asked him about getting the utilities changed. He told her not to worry, they are included in the lease, except for the butane, but he would keep a check on it for her, so she didn't run out. She remembered then that the electricity was mentioned in the lease. They helped her unload her car, putting everything in the hallway, Then they thanked her and took their leave. Bubba wanted to ask her if he could pick up some pecans. The ground was covered with them. But she had already paid them plenty and he thought better of it. "God-damn." Bubba said. "She's sure some kind of weird lady."

"Yeah, she's rich too." his hired man said. "All rich people are weird."

"Yeah, I guess so."

Elizabeth went right to work. First dusting and vacuuming the two back rooms. Then she rolled the ceilings and walls with black paint. By the time she finished both rooms, she had to lie down and rest. She removed all of the silk throw pillows from her bed and laid down, immediately falling off to sleep.

Upon awakening a little after daylight, she fixed a sandwich and drink a glass of milk. She then began to work. She partially rolled out and end from a roll of plastic yard covering, measured the door facings going into the hallway from each room and cut plastic coverings for them. She stapled the plastic from the the edge of the facings, around to the hallway side and stapled it again around the facing on the hallway side so the door would close against it. She did the same thing on the one window in each room. She had to build it around a window air conditioner in each room, leaving only the face of the air conditioner showing. When it came to the transoms over the hallway doors, she remover the handles that opened them, nailed them shut and covered them in the same way as the windows and doors. Once this was finished, she decided that the floor and the doors should be painted. So, back to Lowell's for black floor enamel and a couple of paint brushes. She then painted the inside of the doors leading out to the hallway, both sides of the interior door joining the two bedrooms and their side of the door leading into her bedroom. She then roll painted both wooden floors. Since it had taken her all day and this quick dry enamel should take all night to set good. She moved all of the supplies out of the hallway and somewhat straightened up. Then took a shower, made another sandwich, had a coke and went to bed.

Early the next morning she wrestled the heavy mattresses through her bedroom and into the middle room where she stacked them in twos, put the eggcrates on them and doubled the satin sheets over them, tucked under onto the floor. She then put all the silk throw pillows on them, stacked up toward the back of the wall. She stepped back and looked at the room, mentally congratulating herself for a job well done. She decided to wait on changing light bulbs until necessary.

Elizabeth scrutinized everthing in detail before determining that it was time to go to Romania and bring them back. Yes, it was time, it had been a tedious job, but she was amazed at the short time it had taken to find a suitable place and prepare it. She called Bubba to let him know she was locking the house and taking a trip. She would return in about two or three weeks. She then took a shower, drink a glass of milk and went to bed. Early in the morning she dressed in her new pant suit, packed a bag and headed for the Little Rock International Airport, hoping that she was doing the right thing. *"I better be,"* she thought. *"I'm now deeply locked into it."*

Bubba didn't waste any time in going out to the house to be sure everything was in order. The house was locked up tight. He wondered about the windows on the side of the house being blacked out but did not dwell on it. He looked through the front windows. Everything seemed in order. His main purpose was the two grocery sacks he brought and all the pecans on the ground. He filled each sack about three-quarters full and put them in his truck. He again walked around the house and out to the barn. Her car was gone. *"Vacation."* he thought. *"Hope she has a nice time."* As an after thought he added. *"Weird lady."* He got into his truck, went home and began to shell pecans. His plans were, as soon as he could get them shelled, he would take them to his wife in El Dorado to have for her Christmas cooking. Bubba didn't like staying away from his wife so much. His boys didn't seem to care one way or the other. They had their own thing to do, whatever that was. His wife had told him she didn't want to live in Heaven any longer. She said she would continue to stay with her mother in El Dorado. She wanted him to sell everything and move back to West Monroe, Louisiana where they use to live. He had taken that as kind of an ultimatum pending a divorce. He wrestled daily with his emotions. After all that had happened in Heaven, he knew he would never be able to sell his property. And also—he did not really want to leave Heaven.

Chapter 8

On arriving at the Airport, Elizabeth acquired her ticket and flight number for arriving in Cluj-Napoca Romnia. Her ticket put her back through DFW in Dallas and JFK in New York. She had about an hour and a half until her flight left, so she called Alex and told him about the house and that she had it ready. She gave him the flight number and arrival time in Cluj-Napoca and asked him if he could meet her. She also told him that she would need him to take her around to different licence bureaus and to the newspaper office upon her arrival. *"That will be no problem"* he said. *"I'll be more than happy to see you... I didn't expect to hear from you near this soon."* She then found a beauty salon in the airport, had her hair combed and face made up as she waited.

Elizabeth's plane set down at the Cluj-Napoca airport the following day around 2 o'clock in the afternoon. Alex was there to meet her. He greeted her with smiles and affectionate admiration. They waited for her bag to come down the conveyer into the terminal. She pointed her bag out to Alex. He picked it up, checked the tag numbers, carried it out to the Mercedes Benz, put it in the trunk and asked politely where she needed to go first.

"Let's go to the newspaper office first." she replied.

"We are almost there now." he said with a smile.

"I've written down an article to place in tomorrows paper." she said, as she handed it to him.

About ten minutes later he parked in front of the newspaper office and read her article. It stated: *"An automobile accident yesterday in the countryside took the lives of vacationers from the United States... Mister Harvey Greenstreet... his wife Sarah and their two daughters... Dawn and Mary Jane... were killed instantly... They will be transported home for burial in Heaven, Arkansas, U.S.A.*

"Yes, Miss." Alex said with a grin. "It shall only take a minute or two."

He got out and went into the office. He was back in ten minutes.

"All taken care of. What's next?"

"Alex, do you happen to know of a good forger in town. I need to have passports for all four of the Greenstreets. And documents from a fictious funeral home for embalming, placing the bodies in caskets, crating the four caskets in wooden crates and delivered to Boc-Bella Castle for pick up and delivery to the airport and air lifted to Little Rock, Arkansas U.S.A. With these forged documents I will have invoices and shipping instructions made up for legitimate transfer of the bodies. Once in Little Rock, I shall make arrangements for them to be taken to Heaven. We will put them in the house, buy four new caskets from a surrounding town and have a closed casket burial for the Greenstreets in the Heaven cemetery."

"No, but I know someone that can find one for me. It shouldn't be hard to do, Cluj-Napoca certainly has it's share of the criminal element. Let's go to the hotel and get you a room. I'll have to make a phone call. By the way Miss, Elizabeth— do you mind if I make a suggestion?"

"No, not at all, Alex. What is it?"

"Well Miss, don't take offense, but I would think you should brighten your attire. You know—buy you some brighter clothes. I believe you have somewhat of a morbid complex about working with vampires and believe you have to dress the part and look dark and sinister as most of them do." Elizabeth only looked at him expressionlessly.

Alex took her bag to the room and proceeded to make the phone call, Elizabeth excused herself and went down to the lobby and to the Lady's dress shop where she bought two new pant suits, a light blue and a salmon colored one, two hats to match, and two pair of high-heeled shoes to match. When she returned and layed them out on the bed, Alex looked at them and smiled. "Very nice" he said. He told her the man he called put him in touch with a man to make the documents and gave him a recommendation for me.

"I called him and he gave me the address and told me to come see him about 10 a.m. tomorrow. So I'll pick you up in the lobby at nine-thirty. You look like you could use some rest. You've probably got jet lag."

"Alex, what are you're plans when I get back to Arkansas with them. Or are you going to go with us?"

"Oh no, I'll be staying to take care of the castle. You will be returning with them someday. I'll be here by the telephone if you need anything from this end. Or—if you just want to talk. I'll miss you, you know."

Alex took his leave. Elizabeth had a shower and went to bed. She dropped off to sleep grasping at evanescent aspirations of what a lovable father figure Alex was. But pondered sleepily. Were they the same kind of aspirations Alex held for her????

Morning came early for Elizabeth. By 8 a.m. she was dressed in her new salmon pant suit with the matching attire. She thought she looked to plain so she went back to the Lady's clothing store, bought a little red hat, a pair of red matching patent leather shoes and a pair of red silk dress gloves. She put on the shoes and asked them to hold the salmon ones for her, she would pick them up later. She went to the beauty saloon, had her face made up, her hair combed and the red hat pinned into her hair. Everyone was astounded as to how the red complemented the salmon. She still had time for a bite of breakfast before nine thirty. She was coming out of the restaurant when she saw Alex in the lobby.

"Oh, there you are." Alex said as he stepped back and admired her. "You look absolutely gorgeous."

The little bald man, with thick horned rim glasses invited them into the small parlor at a wood frame house in a run down neighborhood and motioned them to sit at a table in the center of the room.

"We can conduct business here." the man said. "I never allow customers into my workshop. You come highly recommended, so I'll ask you outright what it is you're looking for."

"We need four passports for these people." Elizabeth said as she handed him a piece of paper with the names on it. They will be from the State of Arkansas in the United States."

The paper read: Harvey Greenstreet, age 44/Sarah Greenstreet, age 39/Dawn Greenstreet, age 17/Mary Jane Greenstreet, age 16/Elizabeth was amazed that this man understood and spoke perfect English.

"Will there be more?" the man asked.

"Yes, I will need a document from a fictious funeral home here in town for embalming these same people, placing them in caskets, crating all four caskets in securely fastened wooden crates with three brass handles on either side of the crates. And a bill of laden that they were delivered to the airport for air-lift to Little Rock, Arkansas in the United States."

Elizabeth took note that the man was carefully writing it all down. She told him she thought that would be all she needed. She started to say something else. He told her he did not want to know her name or what she was doing. He said the documents would be ready by tomorrow evening. The price would be one thousand dollars for each piece. A total of six thousand and please bring cash. Come about six o'clock.

Upon leaving the little mans house. Elizabeth looked at Alex somewhat perplexed.

"Now, we've got to get someone to the castle with materials to crate and secure the caskets. Oh, and put the handles on them."

"I'll take care of that. I know just the people that can do it. We'll move them into the foyer and crate them there. I've already prepared the coffins. I put new dirt in them yesterday after you called."

"You what?" she asked. "Put dirt in them?"

"It's a traditional thing with the Boc-Bella's. A two inch layer of dirt from the castle property in the bottom of the casket under the lining. I think it's quite silly. But don't ever tell him I said so. Their caskets lock from the inside, so no one can open them except them."

"Tell me something Alex. How did you ever come to work for Victor since you are not a vampire? I thought you were one when I first saw you. You scared the gee-wheelikers out of me." she laughed.

"I was working as a bellman in the hotel and he came there one night to take care of some business. He saw me, thought I looked like an old movie vampire and asked me if I would go to work for him as his butler, so I did. When I found out he was a real vampire, I wanted to quit. But I'm still here. It's worked out quite well."

"Did he eat at that fabulous restaurant while he was there?"

"No mam, Miss Elizabeth. They don't eat food like we do. They live on blood. Did you get the total house blacked out real good. You can't take any chances on the sunlight getting to them. They are extremely allergic to it. Any sunlight at all is very dangerous and could kill them."

"Yes, I did. She lied, as she remembered the instructions. *"Black out the entire house…God-damn it, Shit"* she hid her emotions. *"I didn't do the complete living room side of the house or my bedroom… damn it to hell… I'll have to do it fast before I have the caskets uncrated."*

Elizabeth remembered to pick up her salmon shoes. Upset, she continued mentally to lambaste herself for not finishing the house. She went straight to the bedroom, fell across the bed, and weeped uncontrollably. The pressure had caught up with her, she knew she had to get control of her emotions and yes—her sanity. She couldn't lose it now. Not over one little mistake. She went to the bathroom and washed her face. She undressed and laid out all her pantsuits on the bed, except the blue one. She put on a robe and called room service to pick up the clothes for dry cleaning. A rush job. She needed them back tomorrow morning early, in hanging clothes bags. She then went to bed and rested. Alex would pick her up at five o'clock to go get the documents.

She met Alex in the lobby after getting prettied up in her blue suit and withdrawing six thousand dollars for the forger and four thousand for her. "*Pocket money,*" She assumed she would be needed a lot of it.

Alex went into the house, picked up the documents in a manila envelope, thanked the little man and then they went back to the hotel restaurant for dinner.

"Shall I take you on your rounds tomorrow?" asked Alex.

"I'll take a taxi. You must get their coffins crated so I can have them picked up, either tomorrow evening or early the next morning."

"Oh yes, I'll make arrangements tonight to have them done in the morning. But you call if you need me. How is your dinner?"

"Marvelous."

Elizabeth's first stop at eight o'clock in the morning would be the Cluj-Monaco airport. Her pressing had been delivered, so she put on the black outfit, feeling it would be more appropriate. Upon viewing herself in the mirror she decided it would not do, it made her look to carefree. She felt that being a family friend accompanying the bodies back home for burial, she should display more of a sense of being in mourning. So, back to the Ladies dress shop, where she picked out a black dress suit with a long skirt, a white silk blouse with wide lace ties at the neck, dark hose, black pump shoes and a small hat with a black lace-net veil. Back in the suite she hanged the pant suit in the closet and put on the new clothes. Admiring herself in the mirror, she was pleased. It now appeared that she could be in mourning.

"Yes—Miss Elizabeth." she said to the mirror. "You do look good."

"My God… I sound like Victor…"

Elizabeth had the taxi driver to wait and was taken to the shipping clerk who in turn showed her to another room to make arrangements for shipping bodies out of the country. She told the man about the automobile accident and that she, as a family friend, was accompanying them home for burial. A lady employee spoke up and acknowledged that she saw the article about the accident in the morning paper. Elizabeth showed him the passports, including hers. The man had the employee to make copies. Elizabeth told him the funeral home here would bring the crated caskets to the airport. The man looked over the passports, copied the names and made out an invoice and bill of laden for shipment to the Arkansas International Airport, in Little Rock, Arkansas, U.S.A. as final destination. He told her to have the funeral people to put them on loading dock number six and for her to check back with him later today for flight time and cost for her and the "merchandise".

Elizabeth was angry with herself and fumed all the way to the hotel, realizing she could have saved two thousand dollars on the documents from the forger. *"get over it… she repeatedly told herself."*

After lunch she called Alex to check on the crating. He told her his two men were wraping it up as they spoke. She filled him in on the details at the airport and ask him if he could possibly get them to help take the crates to the airport. They would need a couple more men to help handle them and an inclosed truck. "I definitely do not want them in an open truck."

"Yes—Miss Elizabeth, leave it to me"

"My God... he sounds like him too."

"Give me two hours, I'll have the truck leaving here with them."

"Good" she said. "When it leaves you swing by the hotel and pick me up. We'll meet them at the airport."

Chapter 9

It was a beautiful sunny mid-day with intermittent clouds as the airplane touched down and taxied to the terminal in Little Rock. Elizabeth Day unboarded and hurried downstairs and out to the freight platform. She had to be sure her freight came off the plane. She watched the men unload the four crates onto the platform. She had her bill of laden and claim numbers in her purse, so she went back into the terminal and claimed her personal luggage as it came down the conveyer and had a porter to take it out to the front while she got her car out of weekly parking and pulled it up to the curb. The porter loaded her suitcases and garment bags into the trunk. She tipped him and drove out of the airport.

Elizabeth, tired and looking somewhat haggard, had been through this same routine three times since leaving Clug-Napoca airport where everything had gone gone off without a hitch. She had the ordeal of changing planes in London, New York and Dallas, with her having to be sure that she and the coffins both were on the same plane.

The black Lincoln went out onto the interstate and into downtown Little Rock where Elizabeth asked a police officer where she might find a large funeral home. She told him she was from out of town and was to attend a funeral and could not remember the name of the home. She said she supposed if she went to any one of them, they could make some calls and find out where she should be. The officer was very obliging. He told her to go to the next light, make a right and go about three miles where she would see a funeral home just past a church.

Elizabeth, gently dabbed her eyes as she mournfully related to the funeral home director, the sad story of having four deceased friends at the airport, which she needed to get to Heaven for burial. Arrangements will be made there for the burial, she told him, but she must have help in getting them there. She told him the whole story of bringing them from overseas and leaned heavily on his sympathy, goodwill and generosity. He devised a plan to rent a u-haul bob-truck that could carry the four crates stacked in it. He would get his son and some of his friends to haul them to Heaven for her. Two of his friends could follow in a car so as to be enough of them to handle the crates. He said his son could pick up the truck and meet her at the airport. He wrote down the freight platform number and she gave him six hundred dollars for the truck rental and expenses.

"I'll pay your son and his friends extra for their help." she said graciously.

"Give me a couple of hours to line it up and I'll have them come to the airport. You take care of yourself Miss Day and good luck. I'm pleased that I could be of help."

"It will probable take me two hours to find my way back to the airport." she said in a mournful joking manner.

Elizabeth had an uneasiness about not being there with the crates, so she went straight back to the airport. She was seated on someone elses wooden box beside the crates when true to the funeral home directors word, in a little less than two hours the u-haul pulled up to the platform. She introduced herself to the four men and gave the airport freight official her bill of laden and claim checks. The men loaded the crates into the u-haul.

"I'll have to go to the parking lot to get my car." Elizabeth said. "So let's meet out on the road and get lined out."

The truck and another car were on the side of the road when she pulled around them and got out of the car. Gathered behind her car, they made traveling plans.

"Do any of you know where we're going?" Elizabeth asked.

"Yeah, we're goin' to Heaven." said one of them.

They all laughed and the man continued "I know about where it is. It's close to El Dorado. I've never been there but I've heard about it. It's where that gas well has been burning."

"Okay, tell you what." Elizabeth said. "I'll lead. The truck will follow me. And then the car. About halfway I'll stop for a quick break. Let's keep close and we'll be fine."

During the entire trip, Elizabeth toyed with the notion of staging a mock closed casket funeral for the Greenstreets, She would need to buy four more caskets and maybe place a couple of cinder blocks in each of them, make arrangements with the local Priest, Minister, Reverend or whoever is in charge of that Church in Heaven to officiate the burial. But then, after much consideration, she changed her mind. After all, who could have possible known them or even cared. She dismissed the notion and spoke aloud to herself. "How stupid."

When the small convoy arrived at their destination, Elizabeth parked the big Lincoln between the house and the butane tank. The truck and other car stopped in front of the house. Elizabeth requested everyones attention at the steps.

"Listen up, men." she said. "We will have to put the coffins in the house until I can make funeral arrangements tomorrow. Now, it 's going to be dark in there. I was preparing for a big Halloween party when I was called away overseas to bring the bodies home and I left the house darkened. What we will do is take them out of the crates, straight through that door into the third room, and set them on the floor. I will pay you handsomely to do this for me."

"Sure." one of the men said. "Halloween's done come and gone, ya'know."

"I know. And I was going to have such a great party."

The men busied themselves with unloading the crates onto the porch. Elizabeth opened the doors and brought back a claw hammer and crowbar from the living room. In record time the men had the coffins in the back room. Elizabeth had them to move all the crating material to the barn, and paid each of them two hundred dollars, for which they were very pleased.

Finally alone with Victor and the brides, Elizabeth felt a great surge of relief and satisfaction sweep through her. Going through the house shutting doors behind her, she went into the back room.

"Victor? Victor?" she called softly. "Victor" she called a little louder.

"Yes, Elizabeth." came the muffled answer.

Elizabeth moved over to the coffin from which the answer came.

"Victor. We're here, but listen to me. This room is blacked out real good. But I want you and your brides to stay as you are for now. I still have to do my room and the other side of the house."

"Is it dark outside?"

"No, it won't be dark for another couple of hours."

"Let me know when it gets dark. I'll get up for a little while. My brides will continue to sleep until I awaken them. I have them in a hypnotically induced trance."

"Okay. That's good Victor. I'll wake you when it gets dark."

Elizabeth pulled off her mourning clothes and hung them neatly in her closet along with her hanging clothes bags of pant suits. She then dressed in an old maroon shirt, a pair of tan slacks and brown loafers from one of her suitcases. She slipped the loafers off and laid across her bed. She slept soundly for three hours.

The bedeviled shroud of evil that had enveloped Heaven since the school burned ninety years ago had now, with the debut of demonic vampires, reinstated it's presence and grown a bit more. A plague brought by the devil to agitate and vex the people of Heaven. There will always be some sort of wicked presence in Heaven to keep it's people afraid, worried, and at bay, as long as Heaven continues to belong to Satan.

Elizabeth heard the inside latch click and watched Victor push the lid up. She watched his face as he raised up, stepped out of the coffin and looked around at her and the other coffins. His expression was that of a young child looking under the tree on Christmas morning. Victor roamed the entire house checking out everything. Elizabeth followed him into her room.

"I plan to begin right away, blacking out my room. Then the other half of the house."

"Yes—of course. That must be done." he said with a smile. "Elizabeth, let me commend you for a job well done. And in record time I might add. Your dedication is much appreciated."

Victor pulled her to him and hugged her tender and lovingly for a long moment before releasing her.

"Oh Yes, by the way." he said. That back door in the kitchen must be secured permanently. It is not to be used as an entrance or exit."

"I'll see to it first thing." answered Elizabeth.

"Yes—that's good. Listen, I'm going out for awhile, to kind of get the lay of the land. Which way is it to town?"

"It's up the road to the left. About five miles. Do you want to use my car?"

She picked up the car keys from her reading desk.

"No, I don't need it. I move quite fast. Almost at the speed of light. But thank you anyway, Elizabeth. I'll return shortly."

Victor went out and eased the screen door shut behind him. Elizabeth opened it and looked out. He was gone.

The back door was easy and only took a short time. She locked the dead bolt, put a couple of extra nails in it, took off the handle and covered the entire door with black double layered plastic. After properly securing the front screen door to her room, removing the handle from the wooden door and nailing it shut, she covered it in the same way as the back door, with intentions of using the hallway door for access to her room. As she blacked out the front window, Victor came in through the hallway door and looked around.

"Yes—this is going to work fine." said Victor.

"I'll finish this room and get some rest. I'll do the other side of the house tomorrow."

"Yes—very good." he said. "One more thing. Secure the front door into the hallway the same as your front door and we shall use the living room door as the only entrance and exit to the house."

"I'll take care of it right away."

"Yes—very good. Then I'll retire now."

His words trailed off as he went through the door toward the back room. Elizabeth began to staple her precut plastic over the side window and filling in around the air conditioner. She had dared to not mention the smeared blood on his face. It looked as though he had made an attempt to wipe it off. She tried to appear nonchalant in the knowledge that Victor had met his first victim of Heaven.

The victim would awaken about daylight, cold, weak, hungry and with a superficial knowledge of what had happened. He knew he had been biten. He knew he craved to drink warm blood. *"How disgusting"*, he would think. But he did not know what to do, or how to start. He had not the ways of an experienced vampire. He was but a novice, a <u>made</u> <u>vampire</u>, with no instructions, as opposed to a <u>born</u> <u>vampire,</u> and he had not yet drank any blood. He knew not what to do, except, he felt the need to avoid sunlight.

The wretched victim would suffer an existence of hate, anguish and mental torture, slinking around the dark alleys at night looking for food and perhaps something, or anything, with blood. And a dark place in the day, like a culvert under a highway. Any place out of harms way of the sun.

All <u>made</u> <u>vampires</u> were destined to become contemptible vulgar low-life's who unwittingly craved the delicacy of warm blood. Their number grew by only one a week, and it wasn't long before there were dozens. They banded together in small groups, black and white, men and women, fighting, cursing and competing for scavenged food and fresh blood, any blood. dogs, cats, rodents, crows and chickens—God, how they loved chickens.

Victor only needed the blood of one victim per week to feed his brides. After taking blood, he would wait two days for the blood to go through a purification process and become pure sweet mineral and protein in his veins. He would then feed his brides from a small vein puncture in his wrist. Each bride dined once a week. Victor was their total source of nutrition. They never drank from anyone else. They would bite someone occasionally, but never would they partake of the blood. So, Victor stayed quite busy, being the sole blood winner of the family.

It had not taken the towns-people long to know they had vampires. Occasionally someone would come up missing. And there were those who, on an overcast day or late evening, would see the naked winged women soaring above them. The people became extremely frightened. They boarded their windows and stayed inside at night. The devil had once again successively maintained his restraint and control over the people of Heaven.

Chapter 10

During the time the house stood vacant, before Elizabeth Day leased it from Bubba. He had a pump house built on to the side of the porch where the hand pump had been, and an electric pump put in, complete with timer and reservoir tank. The water was piped into the kitchen and new bathroom. The bathroom was built between the kitchen and the large living room, taking up it's space from the living room. It had all new fixtures including a tub with a shower. He had a septic tank put in the ground out by the butane tank and plumbed to the commode. Chuck had sent him the money to have it all accomplished. Bubba flirted with thoughts of perhaps moving into it himself. But when the supposed school teacher came along, that bubble burst and his thoughts of living there vanished.

Summer cleaned Autumn's wings with a damp cloth as Spring watched.

"You know." Spring said. "I think I'll go wash mine under the shower."

"That's what I'm going to do too." said Summer.

"Well." quipped Autumn. "Then why are you wiping mine with a rag? let's all go to the shower."

The brides loved one another like sisters and always looked out for each other. They played together, studied together and was each others hair dresser and beautician. They kept no secrets. They were equally obedient to Victor and shared his pleasures unselfishly. They wrote and spoke nine languages fluently, as did Victor. And why not, they've had plenty of time to study and they always enjoyed doing so.

"Victor went out last night before awakening us, so by day after tomorrow our dinner will be as pure as wind driven snow." said Autumn.

Summer asked. "Do either of you remember who's time it will be to partake first?"

"Yes, I believe it's my turn." Autumn spoke up hastily. "Then Spring is the next day. So, Summer, you're four days away yet. Think you can hold out that long?"

"Fuck you, bitch." replied Summer.

"No, no, darling." Autumn chuckled. "Victor will take care of that tomorrow."

It went without saying that Summer meant nothing derogatory about the crude remark. It was only a way they had of expelling ones false prognostications. They all three naturally wanted to be first. It was imperative that Victor have sex while his bride feasted from a small puncture in his wrist vein.

It was two days later at nightfall on the mattresses in the lounging room, when Victor sent Spring and Summer out to explore the town, telling them not to bring back any prey. He would not dine again until the following week. He then opened a small hole in the vein of his wrist. Autumn straddled him, this being the most logical way to keep from hurting her wings, and began to suck his blood. Then began the copulation she had so looked forward to. She dined with short quickened breath and whimpering like a small puppy dog. Her wings quivered and trembled and her toes curled up as she reached her first climax. After three times of climaxic orgasms, Autumn had finished dining and was peacefully exhausted to the point of restful sleep. Victor removed his arm from her mouth and wrapped his wrist tight with a cloth.

The next two nights would be a repeat of the same routine with Spring and Summer and it repeated weekly thereafter. The life of a born vampire and his brides seem to be Heaven sent, but one must remember that they are evil, vicious creatures and disciples of the devil. They like to kind of feel that they are their own boss. Yet they know when Satin beckons, they must do his bidding. For now they are accomplishing what he wants by just keeping the people of Heaven intimidated.

Victor put on his shirt and trousers before going into the living room to talk to Elizabeth. She was sitting in a chair by a small table with a lamp on it. Victor pulled up another chair and sat down facing her as she laid down the book and reached to turn off the lamp.

"No, no." he said. "The light is alright. Leave it on."

It jogged her memory. She had forgotten to replace the light bulbs in their rooms. He reached over and picked up the book. It was a vampire novel.

"I hope you are not believing any of this nonsense." he said with a light chuckle.

"No, but it is somewhat entertaining."

"Yes—I suppose it would be." he said, as he laid it down. "Elizabeth, I've been thinking about your immortality. I feel for the good of both of us, that we should do it as soon as possible."

"I've been thinking about it too. It would protect me in case you backed out once we got back to the castle, and it would protect you in case I decided to run out on you. Leaving you high and dry."

"Yes—high and dry. It would leave me—high and dry. I was trying to say it more delicately, but yes it would leave me as you say—high and dry. I guess our minds think alike. So yes, we will do it as soon as possible. It will take three days of you drinking my blood to effectuate the transformation. You must suck it from a small puncture in my wrist. Only about half a cup each day will be plenty, and you must not eat any of your poisonous food during the three days."

"Damn, won't I get hungry?"

"No, you will not get hungry. You will be digesting the purest nutrition that you have ever had."

"Will I turn into a vampire or grow wings?"

"No, you will not turn into a vampire unless I bite you. If I did that, then we would all be as you say—high and dry—without a keeper. About growing wings. That is not a possibility. That process is much more complicated. Maybe I'll explain to you someday. You know I'll have to make the time to do this and I have only just now started back to feeding my brides. I must continue feeding them for a while before I stop and make them wait. It will take three days for you. Two days for new blood to purify for you and two more days for new blood to start back to feeding them. We are looking at the least of seven days for them to do without. That's why we need to wait and let me feed them for a few weeks."

"Alright, after we are through, and I get hungry. Do I go back to eating regular food?"

"Yes back to regular food. Disgusting,—but yes."

"Tell me, if all Boc-Bella's are immortal. Where are the others. I mean, where are your parents?"

"Elizabeth, immortality is a gift meant for a peaceful existence where there is no violence or vampire hunters to lure you into the sunlight. Sunlight is the one thing that will kill a vampire. Even a Boc-Bella vampire. My parents were killed by sunlight."

"I'm so sorry Victor. Tell me, did your mother have wings?"

"No, not when I was born. I was a young man when she grew them. Many of us are born of brides before they grow wings, but none afterwards. For some reason they cannot conceive once they have wings. I believe it has something to do with the Boc-Bella genes. Throughout the history of Boc-Bella heredity, there have been many born vampires from pre-winged brides. Also, there are many vampire wives who never grow wings. They continue to have offspring and feed themselves. They do not have to be fed by the master as do the brides. They sometimes jokingly refer to the masters brides as concubines. The Boc-Bella clan have always been very loving and passionate vampires. Which reminds me. While you drink of my blood, it shall be imperative that we copulate during your feasting." Elizabeth stared expressionless at him for a long moment.

"Is that a required fringe benefit. Or are you just being nice. Either way, I gratefully accept."

"Yes then we shall start soon. I'm going to retire now."

Victor left the room, leaving Elizabeth with a passionate restlessness in the pit of her stomach, which, as would be expected, the spirit of ol' Charlie and his malicious sexual appetite immediately honed in on. She picked up her book and began to read... *By the light of the moon, the vampire had picked his prey and began to stealthily slip up behind the beautiful young lady. Slowly and determinedly he moved ever so closer toward her...*

Startled, with a heart pounding adrenaline rush, Elizabeth jumped to her feet as the front door opened and Spring looked in. She pulled her head back out and opened the door wide. She and Summer entered the room, returning from their nightly outing. Elizabeth, being engrossed in the passage about the vampire creeping up on a young lady from behind, was relieved beyond words to see Spring and Summer. They hugged her, apologized for frightening her and proceeded to tell her of their outing. "We looked the town over." Spring said. "Wasn't much to see. It's a small place. We did see a few people moving around at one place, going in and out, acting strange and irritated. We think it might have been people that Victor has fed from. Every house in town seemed to have their windows closed shut."

"Yeah." Summer said. "They're afraid of vampires. It's the made vampires from that place that are roaming around over town. We saw one place with two open windows and the lights on. We went to check it out and they shined a really bright light on us, so we left."

"Summer scratched on the window and showed them her fangs." Spring said. "And then they turned the bright light on us. They didn't realize if we wanted to. We could have easily broke right through that window and made them eat their fucking light. But we wasn't looking for trouble."

Chapter 11

The weeks slowly crept by as all had settled into the routine of survival. Elizabeth wondered at times when Victor may get ready to perform the process of her immortality. Victor had been happily fulfilling his obligation to his brides. He had not mentioned to Elizabeth that he had been having thoughts of doubling up on his blood intake so he could continue to feed the brides during the same week he performed her immortality.

"I wonder if I might have erection problems... No, I don't think so, after all I'm only eleven hundred years old....Look at Uncle Lestor," he thought. *"He takes care of six brides and has been at it a lot longer than me... that means for his intake to have time to purify... he has to feed two brides a day for three days a week.... Every Week."*

Victor had always looked up to his Uncle Lestor, but had never wondered why. <u>He now knew</u>. The admiration must have stemmed from his proficiency in the art of sexual love-making.

"Six brides a week."

"Yes..." he thought....*"That would do it."*

Some weeks later Elizabeth had just gotten out of the shower and put on a robe as Spring, Summer and Autumn returned playfully from a nightly outing. They excitedly told Elizabeth about their adventure. They had hidden and watched some Negros, unafraid of the night, having a party at a house where they were going in and out. All the men called each other brother.

"Yo, bro." said Summer, laughing.

"Alright bro." Spring chimed in, high fiving Summer. "Up high down lowaround back." They all jumped around slapping hands and laughing as they went on about how all of them were brothers, and how the women called them all motha-fuckers. They told Elizabeth that they could not understand how fucking their mothers, made them brothers. After telling her all about them. They decided to go back and watch the motha-fucking brothers some more.

"You ladies don't stay out to long." Elizabeth said.

"We'll not be long." Autumn said as they went out the door.

They walked to the edge of the porch and took off, up up and away into the night sky. Elizabeth sit down and picked up the old vampire novel and started to read....*The old vampire with grey wrinkled skin and yellowish-red glowing eyes, held his black cape wrapped up close around his body. His salivating fangs glistened in the moonlight as he crept up behind another unsuspecting beautiful young lady of the night leaning alone against a lamp post. In the dim light of the street lamp he grabbed her, turned her around and sank his fangs into her lovely white neck. He drank hungrily of her blood, let her slide to the ground and slunk away in search of his next unsuspecting victim....*

Elizabeth laid the book on the table as she got up talking out loud to herself "What did Victor call it? Nonsense? yes, he was right." She went to the kitchen and made herself a ham sandwich, got a coke from the fridge and returned to the living room. "*Poisonous food?*" she wondered as she took a bite. Pretty darn tasty though.

Elizabeth was only half through eating the sandwich when the brides came in laughing and trying, with not much success, to mimic the Negros. Spring pinched a small piece of ham from Elizabeths sandwich and tasted it. She shuddered, frowned and spat it out mumbling incoherently. They told Elizabeth goodnight and retired to the back room where they folded their wings around them, crawled into their respective caskets and pulled the lids down.

Victor, awakened by the commotion in the living room, gave the brides time to get to sleep and went into the living room to talk to Elizabeth.

"Yes—good. You're still up. I wanted to ask you if my brides were alright. I heard a lot of noise out here earlier."

"They are fine, Victor. Did they not go to bed?"

"Yes—they did. They are asleep. I was wondering about the noise."

"Oh that. They were playing. They had watched some Negros and were trying to mock them."

"Yes I see. Mocking them. Yes—They would. I saw some of the Negro people when I went out. You know, black people have better blood than white people. Two many white people are anemic, and always full of medication. The black peoples blood is hardy. Lots of protein. And it's sweet, like nectar of the devils. Mocking them huh. Yes they would."

Victor went on to tell Elizabeth about his plan to introduce her to eternal life while he still fed his brides.

"So, when do we start?"

"Yes well, anytime. If you're ready. Let's go to your room." It took no persuading. Elizabeth lead the way across the hall and into her boudoir. Victor took a needle point from a small container which he carried in his pocket. Elizabeth unabashedly dropped her robe and got on the bed. Victor undressed and got on the bed beside her. He rolled over on top of her. A new position for him. She spread her legs as he punctured the vain in his wrist and put it to her mouth.

"You will only need three or four swallows." he told her as his manliness hardened and began to find it's way into her.

"Oh, my God." she screamed subconsciously. *"Oh, yes…yes."*

Elizabeth swallowed blood gagged swallowed more blood thrust her hips upward to meet Victor and moaned in ecstasy with every move. Victor was overwhelmed with the pleasure derived from the different position.

Now, one would know this could not have possibly happened without awakening the sexually immoral spirit of ol'Charlie and causing it to immediately change hosts. The spirit entered Victor and took over. The passionate sex immediately turned to raw aggravated lust. One would not know that except Elizabeth. She certainly knew it and enjoyed every spasmodic tumultuous moment of it, as did ol'Charlie.

Victor only knew he had an extremely bad headache.

From the uncovered transom above the door ajoining the brides lounging room came the excited screams of Spring.

"Fuck'er, Victor—fuck'er, Victor—fuck'er!"

Autumn made her get down and leave them alone. They had heard Victor leave his casket so they had gotten up and went into the lounging room.

When the depraved atrocity, which by any logical standard should be considered sexual abuse if not outright rape, had come to a climax, ol' Charlie's spirit slithered into obscurity turning Victor's body back to him. If, in the realm of earthbound spirits, there may be a shit eating grin, then ol'Charlie certainly had one. Victor, not knowing what had occurred, only had a splitting headache.

Ol'Charlie was surprised to find his new host at it again only about an hour later. This time it was one of his little girl blood suckers. The one he called Autumn. She was straddle him and well on the way to a climax while she fed from his wrist. Ol'Charlie became more intense by the moment. He could not take this wishy-washy copulation any longer. Victor felt as if his brain exploded as ol'Charlie's spirit took over and Victor lost consciousness. What pursued then was no longer amorous love, but instead it turned into wicked vulgar perverted immorality. Ol'Charlie, or Victor as she thought, made her get onto her knees with her wings outspread. He mounted her from behind, violently forcing entrance into her anus. Autumn, in excruciating pain, sobbed uncontrollably while accepting his rough and cruel treatment, not understanding or not complaining. She was his and must accept him, regardless of her feelings. But she wondered, what caused him to do this. Why now, after so many years of righteous virtue. It wasn't at all like Victor. It was like a different person. He finished, got up, wiped the blood from Victor's arm and again slithered into obscurity. Victor regained consciousness standing by the bed with a splitting headache, wondering what had happened.

Ol'Charlie was elated to find that this continued nightly. Elizabeth and Spring, Elizabeth and Summer and then just Elizabeth for one more night. The rough vulgar perversion had continued. It was now time for Victor to, as Spring liked to say, refuel. Knowing it was that time she had gone out at dusk to prowl for a delicacy that might please him. She was in luck, a Negro baby. She was flying away with the baby boy when the mother noticed and began screaming. Victor was pleased and sucked the child dry out behind the house. He thanked Spring and told her to drop the carcus out in the swamp, warning her not to go near that burning crater. He then went out to find more blood.

For the next two days he would go through the purification process. It was like a short vacation where they would lounge around and talk. There was one thing they all wanted to talk to Victor about, but was reluctant to do so.

Ol'Charlie welcomed the lull in the sexual excitement. Elizabeth's initiation into longevity had ended. She was sorrowed. Rough or not, she would take it anyway she could get it.

The brides, when they were alone, talked about Victors sudden change. Summer said she thought he may be possessed by an evil spirit. They all had read about such over the centuries. They knew this place called Heaven belonged to the devil and probably abounded with evil spirits. They agreed that they should try to figure out how to expel the evil spirit from him. They wanted their old Victor back.

Chapter 12

Bubba watched Chuck as he concentrated on the well proportioned breasts of the two young waitresses at the Kings Inn. Oscar paid no attention. He was busy eating.

"You missing your Susie—are'ya?" asked Bubba.

Chuck was somewhat disconcerted to see Bubba watching him. He knew he blushed. He could feel the warmth in his face.

"No, I was just thinking." stammered Chuck.

"Yeah, I noticed."

"What I mean is—yes, I do miss Susie. But that is not why I was looking at them."

"Oh?"

"I was looking at them because—well, do you remember when I was here three years ago. Well, the waitresses that were here then were built the same way. Just like all the young girls in Heaven. If you remember, I made the statement that it must be something in the water, and you agreed with me. Well, I still contend that it's something in the local water that makes them grow like that."

"Man. You sure wiggled out of that, didn't you."

"Do you have a better explanation?"

"No. I don't reckon I do."

"Hey, you fellers bout ready to get down to business." asked Oscar, as he pushed his plate back.

"What business?" asked Chuck.

"You know." he looked around and lowered his voice. "About how to get rid of, you know what."

Oscar made a gesture like he was flying. He leaned in closer and whispered.

"Have ya'll seen the boobs on these girls here?"

"Yeah." said Bubba.

"Yeah." Chuck said. "It's caused by the water."

Oscar looked around to be sure no one was close enough to overhear him.

"I've given it a lot of thought and the way I figure it is. It's got to be the sunshine."

"No, it's the water." said Chuck.

"I'm talking bout the vampires." Oscar whispered. "It's the sunshine. That's what they can't take. I've noticed the windows all are painted over at the café. Probably because they stay there in the daytime."

"Also the windows were blacked out at Grandad's house." said Chuck.

"Yeah." Bubba said. "I noticed that too—oh, by the way, I remembered her name. It's Lizabeth Day or something like that."

Oscar looked astounded at Chuck.

"You mean to tell me there's vampires out at your house?"

"Sheeee. Not so loud." said Bubba.

"I guess so, Oscar. It seems to be. But listen, for now keep it under your hat. I don't want Jim Bob going off half cocked and trying ta'shoot them. I don't think that would get the job done. He would probably get himself killed. I'll figure some way to lure them into the sunshine. I think that will do it. We may have to burn them out of the café on a sunny day."

"Jesus." Bubba said. "Another burning, like long time ago."

"Yeah, Bubba." Oscar said. "But we're talking bout vampires." The two bosomed waitresses came to their table, both with a Kings Inn guest ticket and asked Chuck if he would give them an autograph. Chuck was happy to respond and ask them their names which he wrote on each ticket before autographing it. Bubba and Oscar were overwhelmed with a false sense of importance to be associated with a celebrity. They sat there and stared foolishly at the girls with an uncontrollable grin on their face.

In Elizabeth's bedroom the brides lay across her bed on their stomachs and she sat at her vanity. Victor sat in the bedside chair.

"Yes"—he said. "There's a front moving in from the west and it's going to get cloudy and overcast a couple of hours before dark."

"Or we going out then. Before dark?" asked Summer.

"Yes—I believe so." Victor said. "I think I need to get a transfusion. I'm feeling a little hungry.—And I've been getting extremely bad headaches." The brides looked knowingly at one another. Elizabeth thought briefly about the headaches that she had experienced but said nothing about them. She did however wonder if perhaps her aneurysm could be contagious. But however fleeting that thought may have been, she would never know just how close her supposed aneurysm would be to being her contagious wonderment. If there were a thought or a hormonal impulse to whet the appetite of ol'Charlie's spirit, then that sexual degenerate spirit would most definitely be nefariously contagious.

"It's probably because you've been overdoing it for the past week." she said. "But that's over now. In a couple of more days everything will be back to normal Victor" she said. "This would be a good time to explain to me about the wings."

"Yes—I was going to do that, wasn't I. I will start by telling you that the process takes anywhere from nine months to a year to fully develop the wings. Only Boc-Bella born vampires have the genes to produce a winged bride. He then is obligated to take care of and feed them weekly. They can not feed from any other source. If they were to, they would shrivel up and die. The process of making winged brides has been in existence in the Boc-Bella clan longer than anyone can remember. Now—how it works. The born vampire finds a girl, or girls, he wants for a bride, or brides. He takes her, or them in, and begins feeding her, or them, every five to six days just as he will continue to do for the rest of eternity…."

"I'm assuming you took all three of your brides in at the same time."

"Yes you're assumptions are correct. Well now, in approximately three months a metamorphosis sets in and forms a cocoon on the back covering both inner shoulder blades. This cocoon stays for about five months before it begins to lose it's outer layer crusty skin and exposes the chrysalis. The Greek called the chrysalis a golden sheath. You can see the fully developed wings folded neatly in the sheath. It only takes them a few days to break through the chrysalis and start to unfold and stretch out. Have you ever watched a butterfly being born. That's the way wings are born to Boc-Bella brides. Then the fun begins. Learning to fly."

The brides began to laugh at the memory. They all agreed that Spring took the longest. Autumn talked about how Spring would run into trees and fall down trying to land. Spring said it was hard learning to fly at night. She usually waited for an overcast day until she caught on to it real good. They love their wings. They love to soar through the sky as eagles do. Late in the evening after sundown, they would intimidate the eagles over the castle grounds, with their six foot wing spans. Summer said hers are bigger. She boast a six foot three inch span. It may have taken Spring a little longer, but she learned to fly as expertly as any bird and has always loved the feel of the wind rushing by her face and along her naked body.

It had become extremely overcast and the temperature had dropped considerably by the time Chuck was taking Bubba and Oscar back to Heaven. When they pulled up in front of the court house and parked, Oscar mentioned that it would soon be getting dark.

"Yeah." Bubba said. "We better get inside. And, Chuck. I believe you better stay at Oscar's office with us tonight. It's to dangerous to try to go back to El Dorado."

"You think the flying vampires will be out?" asked Chuck.

"I'd bet on it." Oscar said, as they went through the door.

Mayor Jim Bob came out of his office carrying a three foot long sword in his hand.

"Hey." he said. "I was getting worried about ya'll. You're cutting it real close ya'know. Sandy's not back yet either. She went home to fix supper for us."

"What'cha got there Jim Bob?" asked Bubba.

"This is a silver sword what come out of a walking stick. I was thinking bout melting it down to make more buckshot."

"Let me see it." Chuck said. "It looks interesting."

As Chuck looked at the sword, the door opened and Oscar rushed to help Sandy with the food. They put the pots on Oscar's desk and he went back to close the door. He glanced outside as he heard the noise."

"Bite'er Victor!—bite'er Victor!—bite'er!"

"Jim Bob! git yer gun! hurry up! A vampire has a young boy against a car outside! Ya'll hurry up!"

Oscar grabbed the halogen light and rushed out the door. Jim Bob was right behind him with a shotgun. Bubba hurried into Jim Bob's office and got him a shotgun. By the time he got outside, Chuck had passed Jim Bob and was up beside Oscar. Oscar turned the light on into the face of the vampire who turned his head away from the strong light and dropped the young lady. Chuck immediately rammed him through the chest with the silver sword. The vampire disappeared into the night. Jim Bob and Bubba shot repeatedly at the flying vampires. They both were hitting them with the silver buckshot. The brides were yelling.

"God-damn'it to hell. Don't do that!! That shit hurts!!" yelled Summer.

"You meally-assed bastards, stop it!!" yelled Spring.

"Come on ladies. Let's get away from here!!" called Autumn to her companions.

Chuck picked up the young boy and hurriedly took him into the Sheriff's office. The rest of them came in right behind him. He laid him on Bubba's bed, turned and shouted for someone to bring a wet cloth to help revive him. Sandy came quickly with a wash cloth and began to wash his face and neck. She began to examine him to be sure he had not been bitten.

"This ain't no boy." she exclaimed loudly "This is a young woman!"

Chuck turned back and looked. His face went white. He had trouble speaking. He picked her up and sit down placing her head in his lap as Sandy again began to bathe her forehead and neck.

"This is Susie!" Chuck deliriously blurted out.

"Ya'mean this is your Susie?" asked Bubba.

"Who is Susie?" asked Jim Bob.

"Hell, I thought she was a boy." said Oscar.

Sandy began to wipe Chuck's face with the wet cloth. It helped him tremendously to regain his senses.

"We are going about this wrong." Sandy said. "I believe she is in shock. We need to keep her warm instead of wiping her with a cold cloth. I'm going to get some blankets."

Sandy was only gone for a minute. She brought blankets from her and Oscar's bed. She made Chuck get up and she covered Susie, tucking the blankets in under her. She dried her wet neck and face with a hand towel.

"Does anyone have any brandy?" asked Sandy.

"I might could find some whisky." said Jim Bob.

"That will do. Go get it."

Jim Bob went to his office and brought back a pint bottle of Jim Beam about half full. Sandy found a plastic straw in Oscar's desk. She showed Chuck how to pick up the whiskey with the straw and drip it into Susie's lips.

"Not to much." she said. "You don't want to strangle her."

Chuck pulled up a chair and sit beside the bed with her. He felt helpless and wanted to cry. In his own inexperienced and feeble way he prayed.

Sandy periodically checked Susie's pulse and massaged her arms and hands. She said she must stay warm but not to hot. She told Chuck that her pulse was steady and she would be coming around most anytime. She was worried that Susie may have slipped into a coma but she certainly was not going to tell Chuck that. She knew they couldn't leave here for the hospital before the sun came up and she didn't want to cause any unnecessary worry.

Chuck sat with her throughout the night remembering all their good times and the solemn expressions of love they held for one another. Yes, and the heart-breaking bad times that came close to destroying that love. Like the time he came home with his grandfathers spirit in him. It was a long and sorrowful time overcoming and renewing their love. *"And now this,"* he thought. *"Dear God… if you must take one of us… let it be me. Susie has done nothing to deserve this… I'm the one to blame for her being here. God, please don't make Susie suffer for my mistakes."*

Chuck now realized how the helpless feeling felt, that Uncle Dad told him about, when the Doctor hypnotized Chuck and talked to Ol'Charlie. It's a gut rinshing, heart pounding, agonizing experience that you can do nothing about. Your only recourse is to ask for Gods intervention to save the one you love. And Chuck did. Over and over and over, throughout the night.

Chapter 13

The healing process was effectively swift. Each wound where a buckshot entered the body was healed from the inside out, pushing the buckshot back out from where it entered. In a matter of seconds the brides bodies were like new. Although, it is quite logical that it did hurt and burn from the garlic on the silver buckshot. Victor pulled the sword from his chest and was healed almost as instantly as it came out.

"Why didn't you bite her, Victor?" Autumn asked. "You had enough time." They were in Elizabeth's bedroom telling her about the vigilante attack to save the young woman.

"Yes—I did, didn't I. I was hesitant because I was having an afterthought about something that's been on my mind for a long time."

"What's that Victor?" asked Summer.

"Yes—well. You know I have no heirs. No one to keep my heritage alive in case of my unforeseen demise. So I have been giving thought to taking a wife. And this young woman seemed to me to be a likely candidate. If that is so. Then I must talk to her and be sure before I turn her into a vampire."

They all looked expressionless at Victor for a long while. Spring broke the silence.

"Yeah." she said. "I think that's a great idea. You just run right on up there and have a talk with her."

"Don't act shitty about it, Spring." Summer said. "Try showing a little compassion."

"Yes—well compassion or not. I do need a wife to bear me a son."

"What about Elizabeth ?" Autumn asked. "She would make a fine mother."

"Yes—I suppose she would. But then, she would have to be a vampire, and there again, we would not have a keeper. No, it must be someone else. Someone like that young woman. Elizabeth, I would like for you to go up there in the morning while we sleep and find out what you can about her. See about the prospects of me talking to her. See if she belongs to one of the men there. If so, see about me talking to him. Maybe he would sell her. Riches and immortality, you know, have conquered many a conquest, be it for love or country. Oh, and while you're in town, pick me up some green onions. I have always found that eating green onions helps the metabolism process to build up the blood in my veins and speeds up purification."

"Victor." Summer asked. "Why does it have to be this particular woman. Aren't you taking a big chance talking to them people. You know there are a lot of young women around the countryside. You could easily just steal one."

"Yes—I suppose I could. But this one, well, I liked the way she felt. and yes, the way she smelled."

"I'll check her out for you tomorrow." said Elizabeth.

"Yes—very good. Now I must go out and find more blood. It's time for the late night shift to go to work up at the Oil Mill. I can probably find a straggler there."

Victor went into the back room where he took his black cape from the closet and went back through the living room and out the door.

Crouched atop the front building, Victor watched the parking lot as the workers came in. Just as he expected, he spotted a late arrival. As the man got out of his car, Victor nimbly jumped the forty feet to the ground and was upon the man before he even shut the door. With his black cape pulled around him, like the vampire from Elizabeth's paperback novel, he sank his fangs deeply into the man's neck and within a minutes time, sucked about a quart of blood from him. He let the man slide to the ground and like a whisk he was gone. Victor stood on the front porch for awhile looking at the overcast night sky and thinking about the young lady with the amorous scent of the estrus cycle. For only a moment, his fleeting thoughts disturbed ol'Charlie's peaceful rest. Victor, with the bottom of his cape, wiped any excess blood from around his mouth and went inside.

Elizabeth was eating a sandwich and reading her book when Victor came through the door. She laid the book down.

"Back so soon?" asked Elizabeth.

"Where are my brides?"

"I believe they're in the lounge."

"Yes—well, I think I shall retire. You wake me tomorrow when you return from town."

"I will, Victor."

Victor went through the hall and into the lounge room. He told his brides goodnight as he passed them and went to his casket. When they heard his casket close and the latch click, they went to the living room to talk to Elizabeth. Summer told Elizabeth about their fears of Victor being host to a demon spirit and how the spirit takes control of his sexual motivations. About how cruel and perverted he becomes. They recruited her help in trying to figure out a way of exorcizing the demon spirit from Victor.

The first thing Chuck could think to say was "My God, what happened to your hair." Susie had awakened and Chuck was holding and consoling her. She was still slightly trembling but appeared to be doing well. Sandy was still monitoring her pulse, and was probably more relieved than anyone to see her awake. She had been so worried that she may not come to.

Chuck introduced her one by one to each person in the room.

"You sure scared the gee-whillerkers out of us." said Bubba.

"Yeah." Sandy added. "But I'm sure you've had a fright too."

"I sure thought you was a boy." said Oscar.

"I'm pleased to meet you, Susie." Jim Bob commented.

"You don't try to talk right now, babe." Chuck said. "You wait to you feel like it. Just be quite and rest."

The front passed through during the night and morning awoke bright and beautiful. The majestic rising sun, over toward the direction of

El Dorado, seemed to hesitate for a few minutes and then suddenly pop up with an invincible blinding effect.

Elizabeth was up and dressed, planning her strategy. She figured she would wait about an hour and go to the Sheriff's office. She would ask the Sheriff if he would call Bubba Plunk. She wished to see him to straighten out something about her lease. And if he was still in town, she would like to see Chuck Abbott.

Little did she know she would see them both at the Sheriff's office. When she arrived and knocked on the door, Oscar answered it the same time that Sandy was leaving to go prepare everyone some breakfast. Oscar invited Elizabeth in as Sandy went out the door. Chuck went over by the door.

"Hello, Miss Day. It is Miss, is it not?" asked Chuck.

"Yes, it is, Mister Abbott."

"Did you know about the vampire attack here last night?"

"Why, no." she lied. "What happened?"

"A vampire attacked my lady"

He motioned toward Susie, sitting up on Bubba's bed.

"and became very close to biting her before we saved her. He had some flying vampirettes with him screaming for him to bite her."

"No, Mister Abbott, I knew nothing about it. I came here to see if I could find you or Mister Plunk. I need you to go into El Dorado with me to make an amendment to the lease."

He glanced over to Susie and then to Bubba.

"Sure, Miss Day. Are you ready now?"

"Yes, I am. Please call me Elizabeth."

Chuck went over and whispered something to Susie, kissed her and went back to the door.

"Come on Bubba, go with us."

"But Chuck." Oscar said. "Didn't you say there"

Chuck interrupted him.

"Not now Oscar. Save it for later." Elizabeth, Chuck and Bubba went out the door, to her car and left.

Nothing was said until they got on the new highway 7.

"Mister Abbott." Elizabeth asked. "Is that young lady your wife?"

"Please call me Chuck. Mister Abbott was my father.—No, she's my girl friend."

"I see."

"Alright, Elizabeth. Let's get down to what this is all about. I know you have vampires in the

house. Do you want to tell me about them.—
Were they the ones that attacked my girl friend
last night?" There was a long silence.

Elizabeth pulled to the side of the highway
and stopped. They sat in silence for awhile before
she spoke. Bubba sat in the back seat taking it all
in.

"Yes." she said. "I look after Victor Boc and
his three brides. Victor is a born vampire from
the Transylvania region of Romania. And yes, it
was they that attacked your girl friend. Victor is
looking for a wife and he took an instant liking
to your girl friend. He refrained from biting her
because he wanted to find out the possibilities of
taking her for his wife. He sent me to find out
about her." This struck Chuck as being somewhat
hilarious.

"Well, Elizabeth." Chuck chuckled. "You can
ask Susie if she wants to marry a vampire. But I
believe her answer will be no. Tell me, Elizabeth,
You seem to be an intelligent and sensible woman.
Why are you taking care of these vampires?"

"Well." she said, choosing her words carefully.
"I was kind of duped into the job of being their
keeper. And I was, before I knew it. In to deep
to get out. But it really hasn't been bad. They are
very good people. Affectionate and a lot of fun.

Yes, I have grown very fond of them and enjoy my job."

During all of this, Chuck wondered why his grandfather's spirit had not come forward to talk to him. For Chuck, this was a real mystery.

"Tell me about Victor." said Chuck. "Other than being a vampire. What kind of person is he? Why did he come here to find a wife?"

Elizabeth opened up and gave Chuck a complete rundown on Victor's heritage, his powers and his sudden wish to have a wife to bear him an heir. She explained the difference between a wife and his brides. She told him about the blackouts he had been having, like I use to do, she added. This hit home with Chuck. The blackouts. *Like I would have when grandfather would take over my body. Like when he raped Susie.* Now it all came together for Chuck. Grandfather's evil spirit was now in the vampire, Victor.

Chuck suggested since they weren't going to the attorney to make an amendment on the lease, that they go somewhere for a bite to eat. Elizabeth and Bubba agreed. They went on into El Dorado to the Holliday Inn and got a booth for privacy where they could talk. They all ordered a light breakfast.

"One thing Elizabeth." Chuck asked. "If you could do it over, would you still go to work for him?"

She thought for a little while before answering.

"Yes, I believe I would. You have to understand my situation. I've come to love them, like family. I'll be going back to the Transylvania castle and live very affluently with them. You would probably have to see the castle to understand. Also, I have drank of Victor's blood and became immortal. Victor is over eleven hundred years old, you know."

"No, I didn't know." Chuck said. "Tell me Elizabeth, what in the world is he doing in Heaven?"

"It's just a vacation, to get away for a little while. Listen, if your Susie, it is Susie, is it not?"

"Yes, it's Susie."

"If she was to consent to become Victor's wife. It would take her no time at all to forget this inconsequential and paltry life. She would be surrounded with wealth and live forever. Chuck, if you could be influential in helping her to arrive at a positive decision, I know victor would be more than grateful. Just name a price. Make it in the millions. Or maybe you would like to become immortal. That too, could be arranged."

"Good God Almighty." Bubba exclaimed. "Why would anybody ever want to live forever. It's enough hell just trying to get through one regular lifetime."

"You don't understand, Mister Plunk. You don't grow old like in regular life. You stay young in your prime of life."

"How old does Victor appear to be." asked Chuck.

"I would guess, about twenty seven, or eight."

"About my age." thought Chuck.

They all stopped talking and began to eat their breakfast. Chuck leaned around the booth and motioned for a waitress to bring more coffee. He could not help but notice that she too was well endowed. *"Yes, it has got to be the local water."*

"Elizabeth, you understand I'll have to give this some thought. And I'll have to talk to Victor."

Bubba looked inquisitively at Chuck, but said nothing.

"Yes, I understand." Elizabeth elatedly replied. "Whenever you are ready I'll set it up."

"By the way." Chuck asked. "What about all the other vampires that hang out down at the old café. Are they from Transylvania too?"

"No, only Victor and his three brides. The others are <u>made</u> vampires. They have no powers to speak of. They are worthless inept individuals. The poor wretched souls."

"By <u>made</u> vampire. Do you mean <u>made</u> by Victor?"

"Yes, only as a means of survival."

On arriving back at the Sheriff's office. Elizabeth dropped them off and Chuck told her he was interested and would be there to talk to Victor about noon the next day. "You understand." he said. "I must get all the formalities from the horses mouth, so to speak."

"By all means. We will see you tomorrow."

Bubba looked very worried. He couldn't figure Chuck out.

"Chuck, you're not thinking bout selling Susie. Are you?"

"Don't know yet, Bubba. How much you think she might be worth? Reckon I might could get a couple of million."

"You jerking on my leg, Chuck? It's not funny you know."

"No, it's not. Is it. I want you to go out there with me tomorrow. We've got to figure out a way to evict our borders. And listen, Bubba. Don't say nothing about our talk with Elizabeth, especially about a vampire wanting to marry Susie. I don't think she should know that.

Elizabeth almost forgot the green onions. She turned left off of Main onto South Elm and stopped at the old Ezra Platt grocery store. The store had been refurbished and was being run by a new proprietor. The proprietor or Elizabeth would never know that only a few years ago, the old owner, Ezra Platt, was killed where they were standing looking at the bunches of green onions. On that hapless day, Ezra was standing outside when he saw the flow of immense grotesque swine surging toward him, down North Elm and across Main like a torrential deluge from a broken dam. He saw a few hapless people disappear in blood bathed vortex's and turbulent undercurrents as the raging swine inundated the street and sidewalks. The wild hogs were almost upon him when he ran into the store and locked the doors. The store front plate glass windows disintegrated like wet toilet paper as swine spilled into the store. Ezra felt a strong presence of overpowering evil as he tried in vain to reach the safety of the meat freezer in the rear of the store. He frantically attempted a short-cut over the vegetable bin and screamed in agonizing pain as two large hogs crunched down on his ankles and pulled him to the floor screaming and clawing at the corn and squash. Moving in separate directions the two hogs split him apart like pulling a wish bone at the dinner table. A huge black beady-eyed boar clamped down on the back of Ezra's neck and with two quick thrusting bites, removed his head as other hogs tore away hunks of flesh and gorged themselves on intestines and organs. Some ran out and up the street with parts of Ezra's body while others devoured the fruit and vegetables.

Elizabeth bought six bunches of fresh green onions and headed home.

Chapter 14

Unaware that her affections were about to be negotiated for at the highest level of immortality. Susie sat at Oscar's desk eating a bowl of soup when Chuck and Bubba came in. She looked well and smiled at them.

"Did you get your business taken care of?" she asked.

"Yep, pretty much. We've got to make one more quick trip tomorrow. You know I'm tickled to death that you came to Heaven. And I'm sorry about the vampire incident. But there's one thing I've got to know before it drives me crazy. What in the hell happened to your hair?"

"You like it?" she asked as she reached up and fluffed the back of it. It's really nice, don't you think?" she adulated.

"I don't know. It makes you look like a boy."

"I sure thought you was a boy." Oscar said.

"You remember, I told you they were revamping the show. Well, they are completely changing it. Giving it more sexuality and shock value. They have changed my character from a goody two-shoes to a snooty bitch. That comes about because my fiance' ran away and married someone else. The producer had my hair cut off and restyled and told me to take two weeks off and practice being a little bitch. Chuck, do you think I can effectively be a bitch?" she asked skeptically.

"I'm not touching that one." Chuck said. "But I like your hair, babe."

Jim Bob sat close by in a chair cleaning a shotgun. He spoke up.

"If you want. I could call my ex to come over and give you lessons."

"Chuck." Oscar said. "Come down the hall with me. I want to show you something."

Chuck followed Oscar down the hall past the restrooms to the utilities offices. They went into a room used for meetings and conferences. In the center of the room was a couch which made out into a bed. Sandy had opened it out and brought sheets, blankets and pillows.

"Sandy made out this bed for you and Susie." Oscar said. "She thought ya'll might stay here instead of going back and forth to El Dorado.

"Wow." Chuck said. "This is real nice. I'll have to thank her. Has Susie seen it?"

"Yeah, her and Sandy made it up. They have become good friends. I brought you down here to find out what happened with Miss Day, and what about the vampires at the house."

Chuck clued Oscar in on the discussion with Elizabeth, about Victor wanting to marry Susie and that he had in mind to try and figure out how to rid the house of the vampires. He told him about the difference between the vampires at the house and the ones at the old Argus Barr café.

"Oscar, do you know where you can get some tear gas canisters. They would be very effective in getting the vampires out of Argus's café into the sunlight."

"Yeah, by golly Chuck, your at it again. That's using the old noggin. I bet I can get some from the Sheriff's office in El Dorado."

"Can you go over tomorrow and see about it? Bubba and I are going out to the house and check things out."

"Sure. Now Chuck, don't go getting that pretty little lady of yours married off to no vampire. Damn, I sure thought she was a boy."

"Not a chance, Oscar. But don't say nothing to her about it."

"Okay." said Oscar.

Meanwhile, back at the old homestead. Victor was busy instigating devious plans of his own.

"Yes, you've done a marvelous job, Elizabeth. Hopefully the young man will cooperate and sell me his lady. If not, then I shall be forced to take her even if it means killing all of them. That would be quite easy to do, you know. Although I'd rather be diplomatic about it. Yes—diplomacy and money, should do it."

"When he gets here tomorrow you will have to talk to him through the screen door. I'm sure he will not want to come inside."

"Yes, that's understandable. It is a shame how distrustful people are. But—yes, through the screen. That will work. You did a good job of diffusing the light by painting the screen. It's like a semi-opaque or a semi-transparent. Yes, six of one or a half dozen of the other. I can look through the screen door and see him without the sun bothering me. Yes, Elizabeth, a very fine job. When he comes I want you to go into the lounge and keep my brides there. Don't let them come into the living room. They could be a distraction, and I will need his undivided attention."

"Okay, Victor."

Noon found everyone running out of conversation. Sandy had gathered up the pots and dishes and left for home. Susie had gone to the restroom and freshened up. She looked absolutely radiant. Chuck announced that he was going to take Susie out for awhile. Jim Bob said he too had something that needed to be done. He got up and went out the door ahead of Chuck and Susie. Bubba and Oscar knew Chuck wanted to be alone with Susie so they said nothing.

Chuck watched Jim Bob drive away as he and Susie got into his rental car. He had that same suspicious feeling as before and fought the inclination to follow him. He could not help having that feeling, after all, he knew only to well, the perverse history of Heaven and what it did to it's people. But he quickly forgot about Jim Bob and Sandy. He focused his attention on his new little bitch. He wanted only to feed her, take her to his room, let her shower and show him her bitchy ways.

They pulled in to the King's Inn shortly after the dinner rush had ended and went into the restaurant. One of the bosomed young ladies came over to their booth and asked if they wanted to order or go through the buffet. She looked surprisingly amazed at Susie.

"I know who Chuck is. But aren't you Carla from "The Way Life Turns."

"Yes, I am." Susie answered somewhat surprised.

"What in the world happened to your hair?"

"That's a long story." she chuckled. "You will find out when the new season starts. Chuck, let's go to the buffet."

"Ya'll tell me what you want to drink and I'll bring it for you."

"I want ice tea, sweetened." Chuck said. "What about you, babe?"

"I'll have the same. Thank you, Gloria."

Susie had seen her name tag and was trying to be nice.

"Oh, Gloria." Chuck added as an afterthought. "Bring us both a big glass of water. And forget the ice tea."

"Okay." she said. It is probably better for you."

Susie looked questioningly at Chuck as Gloria walked away.

"You know I figured the sugar in the tea would not be good for you. Anyway the water around here comes from deep artesian wells and is loaded with minerals. It will be much better for you. You should drink a lot of it while you're here." Susie's look turned to admiration as she thought. *In his own boyish way, he does care deeply for me… I've always known he loved me…*

now he wants to see that I get plenty of minerals to keep me healthy."

"Come on." she said. "Let's go get some food."

When they returned to the booth and set the plates down. Susie sit down and drank half a glass of water. Watching her, Chuck couldn't help grinning.

After dinner and signing a few autographs they went to Chuck's room and immediately got into the hot shower. It was Susie who finally said.

"Let's dry off and get on the bed before our skin starts shriveling up."

Sex with a snooty little bitch was as good if not better than with a goody two shoes. Chuck jokingly thought to himself that he would just tell ol' Victor, no deal. He had decided to keep her. They contemplated calling Oscar and staying at the motel for the night. But then Sandy had gone to so much trouble to make them a bed at the town hall, it would be best to go back and not take the chance of causing hurt feelings. Chuck refrained from telling Susie anything about his plans for the next day. He pulled her over to him. "Come here bitch." he said gruffly. She rolled over atop him.

"Fuck you, wimp." she said ever so bitchingly.

"That's the general idea."

What transpired then, Chuck thought would go down in the annals of history, as being the most excitable, enthusiastic and passionate sex ever to exist. It could not be referred to as love making. No, it was sensual, lustful, unadulterated raw sex. When it was all over he had to look in the mirror to see if he might resemble Conan The Barbarian.

By the time they had taken another shower and Chuck had put on clean clothes. (Susie's other clothes were in the Grand Prix rental.) They were almost sundown getting to Oscar's office. Everyone was there and happy to see them. Bubba had been telling stories about Chuck when he was in Heaven three years ago. He had just finished telling about their first meeting in front of Argus Barr's café. He had rushed across the street in a van and motioned Chuck to get in. Chuck was trying to get into the café after his van was blown up when the gasoline tanks exploded at the Texaco station during a wild hog rampage. Bubba related the whole incident in detail. They were all engrossed with the story which ended when Chuck and Susie came in.

"What have ya'll been doin'?" asked Oscar.

Sandy reproved Oscar with a stern look.

"If ya'll want something to eat." Sandy said. "It's here on the desk. Help yer'self."

Susie went straight to the desk and began to make her a plate. She was amazed at how hungry she was so soon after eating the buffet dinner.

"I was just telling'em bout our first meeting. Do you remember it Chuck?"

"Sure I do. How could I ever forget it."

Bubba was elated that Chuck remembered.

"I remember a lot more than the first meeting." Chuck said. "I remember Bubba staying, almost constantly with me at the hospital and helping Uncle Dad cope with the diagnosis of the doctors. I remember him insisting on going with me into the swamp in the halftrack to kill the demon. And I thank God that he did. I would have never came back alive without his help. We went through a lot in that swamp and I'll have everyone know that I'll always love Bubba as my very dearest friend. Only one notch ahead of Oscar. The only difference being is that Bubba and I faced death together in the presence of a monstrous demon from hell. I'm sure that he, the same as I, still has nightmares of that day."

Bubba and Oscar were in tears and had to walk away keeping their backs turned. Susie was about to cry and had to quit eating.

"Who is Uncle Dad?" asked Jim Bob.

Without turning around, Oscar answered him.

"That's Chuck's father. I'll tell you bout him later. Never a finer man lived."

Chapter 15

The beautiful early fall morning, cool, clear and bright, made one feel alive. Susie brought in a suitcase from the Grand Prix and went to the room where she and Chuck had slept. She changed to a pair of jeans, a chambray shirt and canvas snickers. She went to the restroom and very lightly put on makeup, combed her hair, and then went into the office.

Chuck was on his third cup of coffee. He and Bubba sat on Bubba's bed talking. Jim Bob had gone to El Dorado with Oscar, and Sandy had gone home, saying she would be right back.

"Hey babe." Chuck said. "You look like you fit right in."

"Fit in to what?"

"Like one of the local Heaven natives."

"Oh, your referring to my attire. Don't you like it?"

"Yeah, sure. I only meant that you.— Nothing—forget it."

"Okay, it's forgotten. Oh, by the way, I'm going with Sandy today to help her fix dinner. Or should I say supper?"

"Yeah." Bubba said. It's supper. But the way we eat here, I guess it's breakfast, dinner and supper." he laughed alone at his wit.

Chuck got up and went to the coffee pot. Bubba followed telling him to hold up and he would make a fresh pot. As Bubba made the coffee, Sandy came in with a big sack of do-nuts and pastries. She set them out on the desk.

"Hey." exclaimed Bubba. "You must'a went to El Dorado."

"Yeah, thought I'd get something to fill up the empty spaces."

Chuck wasted no time in getting fresh coffee and two do-nuts. Susie, whom normally would never eat such, got her a chocolate covered do-nut and half a cup of coffee. They all gratefully thanked Sandy.

After Chuck and Bubba filled up on do-nuts, Sandy and Susie left to go to Sandy's house.

"When are we go'na leave, Chuck?"

Chuck looked at his watch. Figured the time difference and looked solemnly at Bubba.

"It's ten o'clock. Let's do it. I don't anticipate using it, but just in case. Get a shotgun and put it on the back seat. Make sure it's loaded." Bubba got the shotgun, turned off the coffee pot and they went to Chuck's rental car. Chuck drove as they went down through town past the café and Bubba's car lot, past the empty school house, past the old fairgrounds and was halfway to the house before either of them spoke.

"Exactly what do you have in mind to do?" asked Bubba.

"I don't know, Bubba. Just play it by ear, I guess. My intentions are to make him think I'm interested in helping him acquire Susie for his wife and dicker around on my price for awhile. If Elizabeth was on the up and up and that is really what this meeting is about. Do you remember Elizabeth talking about his blackouts. Well, that makes me think that grandfathers spirit might now be in him. If it is and if I can get his spirit to take over and talk to me, then I may be able to entice him to come outside into the sunshine. Bubba sat and stared at him for awhile, absorbing what he had said.

"Good God-damn. You're sure a conniving son-of-a-gun. You done put a whole lot of thought into this, aint'cha. You're not going inside the house, are you?"

"I don't think that would be very smart. But whatever I do, you just play along with me."

"Okay." *"God, I hope we don't go inside."*

They turned off the highway, drove slowly up the road and stopped some forty feet in front of the house. After sitting there for a few minutes they got out of the car. Chuck went around to Bubba's side and leaned against the car. Bubba picked up a couple of pecans and cracked them together in his hands. He offered Chuck one. Chuck shook his head, no. Just then Elizabeth came out onto the porch. Chuck walked up to the steps.

"Good morning, Chuck."

"Good morning, Elizabeth. Is Victor ready to talk to me?"

"He's inside the screen door. If you are uneasy about coming in. You can stay out here and talk through the screen."

"That would be more comfortable."

"Then I'm going into the back of the house with his brides and leave it up to you and him. I'll see you later."

Elizabeth went inside and the short stretch of silence seemed an eternity to Chuck.

"Hello Chuck, you don't mind my calling you Chuck. Do you?"

"No, not at all."

"Yes—good. Then you call me Victor. Please step up on the porch Chuck, so we can better talk."

Chuck reluctantly went up to the center of the porch.

"Yes—good. That's much better. Now, as they say on television,—let's cut to the chase. Yes,— tell me now. In cold hard cash, how much is your Susie worth to you."

"Tell you what, Victor. Let's look at it differently. How much is my Susie worth to you?"

"Damn old man, if you're there... make yourself known."

"Yes—well I see. Your going to be difficult. But then, how can I blame you. I'm sure she's worth being difficult for. But then, I need her only to bear my children."

"Come on old man... do I have to entice you to wake up?"

"Let me tell you something Victor. I'm sure you've probably had more delectable pussy than any man alive. But you just take a minute and visualize fucking a little minx—my Susie—that is ten times better than any woman or bride that you've ever had. Just think about that for a minute."

Chuck stood there for another eternity thinking it wasn't going to happen when all of a sudden—"

"Hey there Chuckie boy… where the hell you been boy… how you been doing?"

Chuck quickly backed down the steps and out into the yard. He pointed up toward the top of the house, jumped around, yelled and screamed.

"Look up on the house! What is it? Gran-dad, what's that on the house.

Look! What is it?"

Bubba grabbed the shotgun and was jumping around not knowing what to do. Ol'Charlie ran outside by Chuck and looked up on the house.

Now one would have to know since ol'Charlie's spirit was in control of Victor, that is was Victor's body that ran outside into the bright sunshine.

One loud agonizing scream shattered time. "AAGGRAASSSSSSSSSSS."

Then silence as Victor flounced around on the ground. Chuck had a fleeting remembrance of his dad wringing a chicken's neck every time they were going to have fried chicken for supper. He would sprinkle some cracked corn on the ground and grab a chicken while it ate. He wrung it's neck and dropped it on the ground. Victor flounced just like the chicken. His clothes burst into flame and burned off of him as his skin sizzled and burned and his face and hands melted away from the bone. In a matter of only a few minutes there was no skin or flesh left. From the time he started flouncing until there was nothing but bones, an old crazy black crow darted back and forth, cawing and pecking at him. Elizabeth ran out of the house screaming. She turned and ran back yelling at the brides to stay inside. She made them get into their caskets telling them to stay there. Then she went back outside crying. Chuck had grabbed a broom from the porch and swatted at the old crow making it leave. It flew out past the butane tank, circled a few times cawed relentlessly and then flew across the soybean field toward the woods.

Chuck asked about the brides. Elizabeth told him they were in their caskets and would not come out. She told him that they couldn't live without feeding from Victor—only Victor. She told him they were destined to shrivel up and die. In a way, Chuck felt sorry for them. He told Elizabeth he would put Victor's remains in a container for her if she wanted to bury him. She thanked him, went inside and brought back a doubled plastic garbage sack.

Bubba went to the barn, got a shovel and a pasteboard box. They put Victor's remains into the sack, wrapped the sack up and put it into the box.

On the way back to the Sheriff's office, Bubba just stared at Chuck with a big frozen grin on his face.

"I hope Oscar got the tear gas." Chuck said. "We still have a lot of sun left."

Bubba's grin disappeared.

"What the fuck you talking bout?"

"Oh, didn't I tell you about the tear gas?"

"No."

"Well, were going to get rid of some more vampires."

"No shit."

Elizabeth cried the entire time as she ripped back the lining from the bottom of Victor's casket and put two double hands full of dirt into a pan. She took it outside and emptied it into the box under the plastic sack. She then put the box on the porch until she could find a proper place to bury it.

Oscar had gotten eight tear gas canisters from the Sheriff's office in El Dorado. When asked why he needed it. He told them he needed to run a bunch of vampires out into the sunlight.

They didn't question him further, they gave him the tear gas.

"We have plenty of sunlight left." Chuck said. "What say, let's go do it now."

"I'm all for it." said Jim Bob.

"Me too." said Oscar.

"We'll need something to break through the windows." Chuck didn't finish his statement before Bubba interrupted. "I'll run by the house and pick up a couple of axes and meet you at the car lot."

"Alright, let's get at it." said Chuck.

Bubba left first in his pick-up truck. Chuck rode in the Sheriff's car with Oscar and Jim Bob. Jim Bob brought a shotgun. He had gotten to where he didn't go anywhere without a shotgun. Oscar drove the two blocks to their destination and pulled to the side of the street some forty feet shy of the café, cut his wheels sharply and backed up crossways in the street, blocking it. They got out of the car and walked over to Bubba's car lot. In a few minutes Bubba showed up and Oscar got him to block the other end of the street with his pick-up. Bubba brought the two axes and met them on the car lot. "That big plate glass window across the front." Bubba said. "Appears to just be painted on the inside. All we have to do is break it and throw the tear gas in. There's another window in the back, near the back door. It will have to be busted through."

"Bubba." Chuck said. "You and Jim Bob take care of the back. Oscar and I will do the front. Do you know how to use these canisters?"

"Gather round." Oscar said. "I'll show you."

Oscar showed them how to activate the canister before throwing it in. He then told Bubba to only use one canister and they would use one in the front window. That should be enough he said. He wanted to save some in case they found another den of vampires somewhere.

It only took two swings of Bubba's axe to demolish the back window. Jim Bob threw in the canister. Bubba found the back door to be nailed shut. They began to hear yelling and screaming as they went back to the front. Chuck had busted the plate glass window and Oscar had thrown the canister in. The <u>made</u> vampires, men and women, black and white, began to stream out the door into the street coughing, screaming and rubbing their eyes.

They immediately, upon coming in contact with the sunlight, began to fall. They rolled and flounced like Victor did. Their skin and flesh sizzled and melted. Their hair and clothes burned. The sound and stench was ungodly horrendous as they took their last breath and succumbed to the bright sunshine, falling and flouncing on one another. Chuck, Oscar, Bubba and Jim Bob stood in the edge of Bubba's car lot watching the dreadful and piteous sight. Within minutes nothing was left but bones and smoldering ashes. Some were pilled across and on top of others. The best they could tell there were about twenty five. When the tear gas subsided, Bubba and Jim Bob checked inside to be sure there were no more. They didn't find any.

Oscar solemnly said he would ask the town's sanitation department to clean up the mess. Oscar dispersed the onlookers at both ends of the street. They locked the Sheriff's car and Bubba's truck leaving them to block the street and walked back to the town hall. Chuck commented on the possibilities of there being other little pockets of vampires hiding out in other places. He said if these vampires have been going out and biting people and then those biting other people, it could spread like wildfire. Hopefully that hasn't happened.

Once again Chuck and his friends had won out over the evil that permeated Heaven, but they knew it would only be temporary, because they knew Heaven belonged to the devil.

Back at Oscar's office he called the sanitation department and told them about the mess in the street in front of the café. The man he talked to was delighted to hear about the eradication of the vampires and said they would take care of it first thing in the morning. By the time Oscar got off the phone Bubba had a fresh pot of coffee almost done and there were pastries and a few do-nuts left.

"It's been a great day." Bubba said. "Now, to top it off, let's have some coffee and do-nuts. What could be better?"

No one commented on Bubba's jubilance, but they all readily helped themselves to the pastries and coffee, before they voted unanimously to lay down and rest, or maybe even take a nap. Each of them went to their respective sleeping place and stretched out.

Chapter 16

Susie laid propped up on one elbow beside Chuck, lightly and lovingly stroking his forehead with her fingers and gingerly, so as not to wake him, she kissed his cheek. He did however awaken when she softly whispered her love for him. He pulled her to him and kissed her long and affectionately.

"We brought some dinner." she said. "Don't let it get cold."

"I'm trying not to." She pulled away from him.

"Get your ass up and go eat."

"Alright, don't get bitchy. You were doing so good." She laughed at him and got up.

"Yeah, but you know I have to practice at being bitchy. Come on, it's after sundown already."

"It don't make any difference. There aren't any more vampires."

"Where did they go?"

"We killed them."

Susie was astonished and she paled at the thought of them fighting vampires. They could have been bitten or killed.

"My God, sweetheart. I thought you had been asleep all day."

She put her arms around him and hugged him tight. Thankful that he was alive. She almost cried, but managed to hold it back.

"Let's go eat and you tell me all about it." she said. "You killed all of them—my God!"

Oscar, Bubba and Jim Bob fixed them a plate and sit down to eat. Chuck and Susie came in and Oscar got up from his seat at his desk and made Chuck take it. He then poured Chuck a cup of coffee.

"I'll tell ya'll something." Oscar said. "This here man is my hero. He come up with the most ingenious plan for getting rid of the vampires. Just like he did to get rid of the demon and the hogs."

"Talking bout ingenious." Bubba said. "You should of seen him at work out at the house where he killed ol'Victor. That's the one what almost bit you, Susie."

Oscar and Bubba, with Jim Bob jumping in occasionally, went on to tell Sandy and Susie how they eliminated all of the vampires, except, Bubba said. "The three with wings." But Elizabeth said they were going to die, because they no longer have Victor to feed from. Sandy asked Bubba to explain what he was talking about.

"I don't understand it either, Sandy." Bubba said. "I'm just telling you what she said."

"How would she know that?" asked Susie.

"She was Victor's and the three winged girls keeper." Chuck said.

"Keeper?" asked Susie.

"Yeah." Chuck said. "Like in the movies. You know, they all had keepers to look after them. The three winged girls were his brides."

"All three of them?" asked Susie. "Good Lord."

"Yeah." Oscar said. "He sure knew how to live, Hell, he was even looking for a wife."

Chuck coughed to break up the talk and gave Oscar a stern look. No one noticed or asked Oscar what he meant. Bubba started talking about how Chuck tricked Victor out into the sunshine and how he sizzled and burned. Chuck told them how it reminded him of his Dad wringing a chicken by the neck and how it flounced on the ground, just like Victor did. He made it sound amusing but he sure wasn't amused watching him die. On the contrary, he was scared and tremulous. As was

Bubba. And he wondered about the spirit of his grandfather. And yes, also the spirit of Victor.

Even after being host at one time to his grandfather's spirit, he still could not fully comprehend the movements or machinations of spirits. He did not care to dwell on it, just so long as he knew his grandfathers spirit was not again with him. He didn't think it would be. He had shown him vivid scenes in his mind of the priest, with crucifix and holy water, exorcising the demon from Linda Blair in the movie, "The Exorcist". He felt the fear in him and he knew if he ever entered him again, the exorcism would happen to him. No, he didn't think it would ever happen again. His grandfather was to smart to take that kind of chance.

"What say, lets all walk downtown and look at the vampire bones." Sandy said. "It's only two blocks."

"Yes, let's." Susie said. "I'd like to see them."

"I'm game." Jim Bob said. "Let me get my shotgun."

"Ya'll just hold up a few minutes till me and Chuck get through eatin'." said Bubba.

"Jim Bob, you got a flashlight?" Oscar asked. "It's done got dark."

"Yeah, I'll bring one. You have your's?"

"Yeah."

Chuck held Susie's hand as they walked out to the street. Suddenly, without any forewarning, a humongous grey wolf sprung atop a car and leaped high in the air toward Chuck and Susie with a gut wrenching loud growl. Chuck's impulsiveness and fast reflexes made him grab Susie and hurl themselves to the side, falling away from the animal. Jim Bob immediately shot the wolf in mid-air. It made a horrendous sound and fell to the ground whimpering mournfully like a wounded dog. In a few anguishing minutes the big wolf succumbed to a problematically welcomed death. Oscar and Bubba held their flashlights on it as they all gathered around looking at it.

Susie trembled uncontrollably and started crying. Sandy put her arm around her and told Chuck she was going to take her inside. Chuck went inside with them to comfort Susie. Oscar, Bubba and Jim Bob watched in awe as the dead wolf began a metamorphosis like transformation. Within about five or six minutes the wolf became a human being. Lying before them was a large naked man with a shotgun blast through his upper right ribcage.

"It was a damn werewolf." Jim Bob said. "A damn werewolf."

Oscar was struck speechless. He was mumbling incoherently.

"Oscar." Bubba excitedly said. "Go get Chuck. Tell him to come out here." Oscar came back with Chuck.

"Chuck, take a good look at this man. Do you recognize him?"

"Yeah, Bubba, it's Milton Parker from the oil mill."

They all continued to look at the man as they heard the far away howling of another wolf. They looked knowingly at one another as Bubba pointed up to show them the full moon.

Back inside, they all decided not to go back out before tomorrow. Susie was much better and said she felt fine. "It was just the sudden derangement of my mental capacities." she said jokingly.

"Jim Bob." Chuck said earnestly. "I certainly thank you for being so quick witted in shooting that werewolf."

"Thank you, Chuck. I'm just glad to know that my silver buckshot was good for something."

"Sandy, I'd like for you to let Susie hang with you tomorrow. I need to go out to the house and see Elizabeth about Victor's brides. I need to know what her plans are."

"Sure, Chuck." Sandy said. "She can stay with me. I'll enjoy her company. I'll help her work on her bitchy attitude."

"Ya'll know." Bubba said. "One thing we got going fer us. We only have to worry bout the werewolfs one night a month. When we have a full moon. Not like the vampires."

"Yeah, that's right." Oscar said. "Chuck, what'cha gona' do bout them other three vampires?"

"I don't know yet Oscar. But I'll think of something."

"I know you will, Chuck. You're good at that."

Chuck had no way of knowing that his delima was in the process of being rectified as they spoke.

Nervously and about to cry. Elizabeth pleaded. "Can't we try to figure out something. I love you."

"I know, Elizabeth." Summer said. "We love you too. But you must realize what will become of us, and certainly you don't want that. We would be horribly sick until we wasted away. What we have planned is what we must do. In a while you will be glad for us."

"When do you plan on doing it."

"Right now, Elizabeth. There is no use in postponing the inevitable."

Elizabeth hugged each of them affectionately and walked out on the porch with them, trying her best to hold back the tears. Summer picked up the box with Victor's remains and they took off up into the bright night sky. They gained altitude, turned and headed out over the swamp. They saw the light from the fire and flew toward it. When they got over it they folded their wings and dropped. There would be no one to witness the sad ocassion of the three beautiful brides combust, like bugs over a campfire, and drop into the roaring bowels of hell.

Sometime before daylight, Elizabeth had composed herself and called Alex at the Boc-Bella castle. She knew she must report the happenings to him. Only three rings and Alex answered the phone. He was overjoyed to hear her voice. He knew however that something was amiss or she would not have called. She explained everything in detail, telling him about the brides suspicions of an invading demon spirit in Victor. They had concluded that is was this evil spirit that caused him to run outside into the sunshine. Then she told him about the burning crater out in the swamp and the brides decision to drop into it instead of going through an agonizing slow death. She told him they took Victor's remains with them. Elizabeth couldn't help but start crying again and had to stop and compose herself. Alex had listened intently and not said a word. He felt extremely sorry for her and for the loss of Victor and the brides.

"Elizabeth, you take some time to pull yourself together and wrap things up there. And then you come home to the castle. Tell me, did you ever drink of Victor's blood. To become immortal?"

"Yes." she said. "But Alex, will I be able to continue living at the castle with Victor gone."

"By all means. It is your home. Before leaving, he turned over power of attorney to me and left me in control of the Boc-Bella estate and all Boc-Bella holdings. Yes, Elizabeth. This is your home, and by the way. I too, am immortal, and like you, I am not a vampire. I became immortal long before you and I ever met. In all reality I was Victor's keeper."

"I don't know what to say Alex. You're so full of surprises. I'm completely astounded. Listen, I feel that I should put this house back in order before I leave."

"Whatever you need to do. Just let me know when your plane will arrive and I'll pick you up. Oh, you may not recognize me, I've had orthodontic surgery. I no longer have an overbite or the two big front teeth. I now look like a human being. They implanted all of my new teeth, the last ones were put in a couple of weeks ago. The dentist will be removing the last of the little wires hanging from my mouth in a couple of more days. And I never opened the castle for tourist either. I removed any signs of there ever being vampires here, but I told the tourist bureau I would not allow strange people going through the castle. There are just to many valuable treasures here to take a chance on strangers defacing them."

"Okay. It will take me awhile Alex, but I'll be calling you."

Chapter 17

Oscar was up early and called an ambulance from El Dorado to pick up Milton Parker and take him to the morgue. He waited awhile for what he dubbed normal people to start work and called personel at the Ouachita Oil Mill. He told them about Milton Parker and where he was. Chuck came into the office fully dressed to see if he could help with anything. He poured himself a cup of coffee and looked through the do-nut sacks. There wasn't any left.

"You want me to send Sandy for more do-nuts." asked Oscar.

"Naugh, I need to get on out to the house and talk to Elizabeth Day.

You want to go with me Bubba?"

"Sure."

"Bring a shotgun, with silver buckshot. You just never know when we might need it."

"Take notice down the street." Oscar said. "See if they have started the cleanup yet."

"Okay." Chuck said as he and Bubba went out the door.

Bubba laid the shotgun on the backseat of Chuck's Plymouth rental car. They got in and drove down Main, almost to the Sheriff's car. There were some men with shovels and garbage cans cleaning up the street. Chuck turned left on South Elm, drove past the Drug Store, Long's Hardware and the grocery store, which still conducted business as Pratt's Grocery. He made a right and drove two blocks, made another right and went back to Main, turned left across from the desolate and ghostly Elementary School, continued on to where he intercepted the old Highway 7, made a right and proceeded to the turnoff taking them to the old homeplace.

Elizabeth, her eye's red and swollen, met them on the porch. She asked them into the living room. They reluctantly went in and sat down. She sat by her reading table and related in as much detail as possible what had happened with the brides and explained to Chuck again why they elected to end it last night. Chuck could visulize the saddening scene of them dropping into the inferno. *"My God,"* he thought. *"Into the pit of hell, where the demon and all of the evil spirit infested swine went."*

Elizabeth told them she would get the house back in order and then she would leave. She told them she would just forfeit on the lease. As an after thought she told Bubba if he would help her with the house and burn the empty caskets that she would sign over the Lincoln to him, providing he would take her to the airport. Bubba glowed with the thought of owning the Lincoln.

"Sure." he said. "I'll be happy to help."

"Where are you going." asked Chuck.

Chuck noticed a tinge of exuberant joy when she said she was going back to Romania.

Feeling that they needed to, or should, be assured that the brides were gone, she took them through the house into the back room and showed them the empty caskets.

"Wow." Bubba said. "I could probably sell these."

"No, Mister Plunk, I really want them burned."

"Yeah, okay." Bubba said disappointedly. "I'll burn'em. That'll be easier to do anyway. How bout I come back this afternoon and get started. I'll bring my handyman to help."

"Okay, that will be fine. I'll pay your man for his help."

Bubba only smilled. He felt like some kind of highway robber.

On the way back to the office they saw the street was cleaned. Bubba got out, moved his truck onto his car lot and got back in the car with Chuck. Chuck maneuvered the car around the Sheriff's car and drove to the town hall.

"Oscar." Bubba said as they entered. "You can get your car. The street is all cleaned up."

"Good. I'll walk down and get it after awhile. We been talkin' bout sending Chuck and Susie on home. Jim Bob say's we can handle the werewolf thing by ourselves, since it'll just be one night a month."

"Sounds good to me." Chuck said. "Susie has to go back to work soon and that'll give us a few days alone. But listen now, if anything else unexpected happens, you call me and I'll be here."

Chuck noticed Bubba wasn't saying anything. He sat glumly on his bed and looked dejected.

"Oh, Bubba." he said. "I'm counting on you partner. When you take Miss Day to the airport, be sure to call and let me know. And get the house back in shape to rent."

Realizing he was needed and depended on, Bubba perked up but was still saddened about Chuck leaving. He got up and poured himself a cup of coffee. Sandy poured another cup and gave it to Chuck.

"What happened about the three brides?" asked Susie.

"I was beginning to think nobody cared." said Chuck.

"Sure we do." Jim Bob said. "It's just they we're all concerned bout getting ya'll home."

So Chuck related the whole heart-rending story about the beautiful young ladies flying over and dropping into the inferno. He covered every minor detail, even adding a few extras to make it more grievous and pitiful. When he finished, Sandy and Susie were crying. Bubba may have been, he was over by his bed with his back to everyone. Could be, he was laughing.
Chuck told Oscar, Jim Bob and Bubba that he saw a logical place for more vampires that would warrant being checked out. If there isn't any there, then there shouldn't be anymore. Be sure no one goes alone. Stick together and take every precaution."

"Where?" asked Oscar.

"The vacant schoolhouse." said Chuck.

They all looked at one another and nodded their heads.

"But then." Chuck continued. "If recent movies I've seen are correct. As legend has it, the werewolves will take care of any remaining vampires."

Susie had packed her suitcase and put it into the Grand Prix. All of Chuck's belongings were at the motel. They all said their goodby's. Bubba walked out with them. Susie told Chuck she would follow him and she got into the Grand Prix.

"Oh, Bubba." I saw that silver sword in the living room. Would you see that Jim Bob gets it back."

"Yeah, sure." said Bubba. He grabbed Chuck and hugged him like he didn't want to let him go.

"I love you too, partner." Chuck said. "I'm sure I'll be back someday. In the meantime, you be sure and call me."

Chuck got in the Plymouth and headed east toward highway 7. Susie followed him.

When they arrived at the motel, took a shower and put on clean clothes. It was lunch time.

"Hey, babe. I'm sure there must be an Enterprize rental in El Dorado. I can turn in the Plymouth and ride to Shreveport with you. What say, let's eat some lunch. And you can drink a lot more of that good water."

After lunch they acquired directions to the rental agency, put Chuck's luggage in the Grand Prix, turned in the Plymouth and headed for Shreveport to get a flight to LAX. While on the road, Susie reluctantly told Chuck that Sandy was having an affair with Jim Bob. She said she had seen the signs. The way they looked at one another and secretly communicated behind everyone's back. She told him how she hated to tell him, with Oscar being his good friend, but thought he might ought to know. Chuck looked expressionless at her and never commented. He did however ask her to remind him to send the King's Inn Restaurant a personal autographed 8x10 glossy. And then he asked solemnly.

"Susie, will you marry me?" Several years together. One stretch of bad times three years ago and marriage had never been mentioned. Either of them had no doubt of their love for one another. The situation with Victor wanting her for his wife got Chuck to thinking. *What if others, or anyone, may want her. I have no claim on her. No way to categorically say, NO, she's mine.* Susie, shocked, only stared at him. He looked over at her. She saw the sincerity in his face. "Certainly, Chuck." she was about to cry. "You know I'll marry you."

Nearing mid-day the previous morning, across the soybean field from the butane tank, deep into the woods along an un-used grown up road. Old Booger Jim sat on his porch in his chair. The rundown antiquated two room shack with a washtub on the front porch. Surrounded by a fence fortified with old rotted lumber, logs and wire, had not changed much in three years. Hanging around the fence at about one foot intervals were large bunches of garlic. Beside the front gate sat an old rusty antique flatbed truck permeated by an undergrowth of saplings and briers. In the side yard was a garden saturated with fall turnips. Sitting on a low cane bottom chair, peeling and eating a raw turnip was the old small black man with bushy white hair and crudely cropped white beard. His dirty faded bib overalls and worn out over-sized brogans accentuated by a necklace of garlic, gave him an air of diabolical eccentricity.

As Booger Jim ate his turnip, an old black crow fluttered down and alighted on the railing alongside his porch. The old man picked up his homemade walking stick and started to hit the old crow which sit only about four feet in front of him. The old crow turned it's head from side to side and started cawing erratically. The old man leaned in closer to the old crow and peered studiously into it's eye. The old crow continued to caw as if trying to tell the old man something. The crow leaned it's head to the side and looked at the old man with the one eye that the old man was peering into.

"Charlie? Is that you, Charlie?—Charlie?" The old crow kept looking at him and again started the erratic cawing.

"Charlie! That is you! Booger Jim knowed it's you, Charlie! How'd you git stuck in that old crow, Charlie?" Booger Jim laughed uncannily while slapping his hands against his legs.

"And you thought Booger Jim's crazy! Didn't'cha Charlie? Everbody thinked Booger Jim's crazy!— But Booger Jim ain't stuck in no crazy old crow." Booger Jim again started slapping his leg and laughing loud and uncannily.

Exactly two months had passed when Bubba finally called Chuck. Not reaching him he left a long message on his answering machine. Susie had been back to work for six weeks and her show was doing great. The Hollywood trade papers were giving it dynamite reviews and praising the story changes. Chuck had again performed at the Troubadour. Pete Anderson recorded the entire performance with aspirations of putting out a CHUCK ABBOTT, THE THIRD album, LIVE AT THE TROUBADOUR. But he still wanted to do a lot of studio recording for future albums. There was a major theatrical movie in pre-production which Chuck had been cast in as co-star with two super-stars. He and Susie plan to be married immediately after Chucks movie wraps.

Bubba's message said he had returned home from taking Elizabeth Day to the Little Rock airport and seeing her off. He said he now owned the big Lincoln Town Car and the house was in good order. After he, Elizabeth and his helper put it in shipshape, she hired a painting contractor to bring in a crew and completely redo the inside in all light colors. Then they got all of the furniture in from the barn. They are coming back next month he said, to scrape and paint the outside. Elizabeth, he said, was a real good worker, she stayed with us through the whole thing. All of my spare time for the next few months will be spent shelling pecans. Ha Ha. And no, we've not found any more vampires.

Jim Bob has been out on two full moons with his shotgun. He heard a werewolf both times, far away, but hasn't killed any more. Everything seems to have kind'a settled down. Oscar and Sandy said to tell'ya hey.

Epilogue

It was 11 a.m. at the Cluj-Napoca airport when Alex met Elizabeth's plane. Alex approached her in the boarding lounge when she came out of the ramp from the plane. She did not recognize him. "It's me." he said. "Alex." She was flabbergasted beyond the realm of stupefaction. It took her awhile to regain her senses before she could speak. In front of her stood a completely different man than the Alex she had known. He was an extremely handsome middle aged man with a young Clark Gable style mustache. His graying sideburns only complemented his good looks. All she could say when she regained her composure was "My God, it's really you."

Alex suggested they stop at the hotel for lunch. Elizabeth recounted in detail the events of Victors sudden demise and of his brides decission to forego a drawn out sickening and painful death. She told him about their belief that Victor was possessed by an evil spirit and that was what caused him to run out into the sunlight.

Elizabeth began trying to hold back a sudden emotional outbreak of sobbing. Alex moved his chair over to where he could appease and comfort her. They both loved Victor and his brides like members of a family and knew they would forever miss them. In a little while the sobbing subsided and Elizabeth, after much consideration, had determined that she should tell Alex of her condition before getting settled into the castle. She feared what his reaction may be. "Alex, I'm pregnant with Victor's child." she blurted it out and waited solemnly for his response. He stared unexpressively for a few moments before responding. "That's great. Is it a boy or girl?" To ease the tension, she remarked "Yes, I'm sure it's one or the other." They both laughed. "How far along are you?" he asked. She thought for a moment, counting on her fingers. "Two months and two weeks. I haven't seen a doctor yet." Alex showed a slight expression of concern. "We'll have to take care of that right away." he said.

Alex made the appointment and took her to the doctors office. They left with a multitude of instructions and booklets on pre-natal care. Alex was enthusiastically excited, as if he were going to have the baby. They decided on which room would be the nursery and how it would be arranged. Alex read all the booklets and helped Elizabeth to follow the instructions. Properly balanced and nutritious diet. Folic acid and iron supplements. No junk food. No tobacco or alcohol and get the right amount of daily exercise. Sometime during the second trimester of the pregency, through the means of ultrasound scanning, the doctor determined the gender of the baby. "It's a girl." he said. Alex's blank look of wonderment turned to a humongous smile. He leaned over the examination table and kissed Elizabeth.

Then came the name game. No name sounded good enough for Victor's daughter until Elizabeth decided she would be named after her step father, her birth father and with her hereditary family name. And so, her name would be recorded as: **Alexandra Victoria Boc-Bella**. Alex's eyes teared as she announced the name. He was glad she would not be stripped of her family name. As he had told Elizabeth, she would have relatives scattered in towns and villages throughout the mountainous areas of the northern Transylvania Region.

He reminded her that "Vicky" as he dubbed her, would be a nocturnal person and in order to accustom her to such would require a different upbringing than ordinary children. He also casually mentioned, in order of proper family appearances, that they should be married. Elizabeth took it as a proposal and readily said "Yes, I will."

"I think we shall raise her as a non-practicing vampire." said Alex. *"Yeah… right."* Elizabeth thought. *"If she takes at all after her father, I'm sure she will do as she damn well pleases…. "*

"Darling." Alex said. "May I call you darling?"

"Certainly."

"Let's go home and watch "The Way Life Turns" It's really gotten good since the hiatus." he said. "Then what say let's go out for lunch."

"I'm game—darling."

the end

About The Author
(In a nutshell)

Jim **Feazell** retired filmmaker and singer-songwriter worked in Hollywood for twenty-two years as a motion picture and television stunt actor. After retiring from stunt work, he headed his own film production company for fifteen years in El Dorado, Arkansas. Tucson, Arizona and Hollywood, California. He wrote many screenplays which included "Time And Time Again"/"Two Guns To Timberline"/'A Deadly Obsession"/"Redneck Mama" and "Wheeler" which he Produced and Directed. Former affiliates; SAG/AFTRA/DGA/MPAA/WGA-W/MPSA.

Now, retired from Motion Picture Production. He has become a novelist. This book "Return To Heaven" is his fifth. It is a sequel to his first book "Come The Swine" All of Jim's books are Supernatural Thrillers and/or Mysteries.